The MYSTERY of the
DANCING
DEVIL

"That's the thief," whispered Jupiter Jones. "Quick, let's get the police!"

But just as the Three Investigators stepped out of the shadows, there was a blinding flash, and an unearthly shriek filled the air!

Then, from a cloud of smoke, appeared a huge, inhuman creature. It moved slowly toward the boys, its menacing face snarling.

"Beware! Be warned! Do not seek the sacred statue. Those who defy us are destroyed!"

Alfred Hitchcock

and The Three Investigators in

The MYSTERY of the DANCING DEVIL

Text by William Arden

Based on characters created by Robert Arthur

Random House  New York

The Mystery of the Dancing Devil

Originally published by Random House in 1976
First Random House paperback edition, 1981

Library of Congress Cataloging in Publication Data

———————.

   Alfred Hitchcock and the three investigators in
The mystery of the dancing devil.
   ([Alfred Hitchcock and the three investigators series]   ;   25)
   SUMMARY: The Three Investigators search for a stolen statue only to
find that it has mysteriously come to life.
   [1. Devil—Fiction.   2. Mystery and detective stories]   I. Arthur,
Robert.   II. Title.   III. Title: Mystery of the dancing devil.
[PZ7.L984Ag 1981]   [Fic]   80-29350
ISBN 0-394-84862-4 (pbk.)

Also available in Gibraltar Library Binding

Manufactured in the United States of America
   1   2   3   4   5   6   7   8   9   0

Contents

A Word from Alfred Hitchcock

Greetings, mystery lovers!

Once again I have been called upon to introduce that trio of formidable young detectives known as The Three Investigators. And again I find myself forced to admit that their latest case is worthy of your attention. Seldom have I heard a tale that possesses greater historical scope than this one—which ranges from the barbarous hordes of the great Genghis Khan to a group of sophisticated modern-day conspirators. And seldom have I encountered a more bizarre case. In the course of reading this story, you will meet the monstrous figure of the Dancing Devil—the eerie sight of which is guaranteed to chill your blood!

But lest I be carried away, allow me to proceed with the formal introductions. Jupiter Jones, the stout First Investigator and mastermind of the junior detective firm, is relentlessly determined in the pursuit of a mystery, no matter where it might lead. Pete Crenshaw, the athletic Second Investigator, is more wary of confronting danger, but always dauntless when his help is needed. Bob Andrews, quiet and studious, is in charge of Records and Research, a duty he performs meticulously. All three chaps live not far from Hollywood in Rocky Beach, California, where they maintain a secret headquarters . . . but you will find out for yourself soon enough. Suffice it to say that the lads' combined talents have enabled them to solve some very unusual cases indeed.

And now, if you have the courage to meet the Dancing Devil, you may turn to Chapter One and commence reading.

ALFRED HITCHCOCK

The MYSTERY of the DANCING DEVIL

1

The Flying Doll

"You're detectives," the little red-haired girl said eagerly. "You can find Anastasia! I want to hire you!" She held out fifty cents in her grubby hand.

Pete Crenshaw laughed. "We don't look for dolls, Winnie."

"Our cases are somewhat more important, Winifred," added Jupiter Jones.

"Anyway"—Bob Andrews grinned at Pete's six-year-old neighbor—"I'll bet you lost your doll right in your house."

"Sure." Pete laughed. "You go home and look some more, Winnie. We have to take my dad's movie projector to be fixed."

The three boys, known throughout Rocky Beach, California, as the junior detective team of The Three Investigators, had been spending the first morning of spring vacation straightening up the Crenshaw garage. They had just finished, and were about to take Mr. Crenshaw's movie projector to the repair shop, when Winifred Dalton pushed through the high hedge from next door and requested their help.

"We're sorry you lost your doll," Pete went on, "but my dad wants his projector in a hurry. We've got to go, Winnie."

"I didn't lose Anastasia! I didn't," Winnie cried. "She flew away. She was in her bed in the yard, and she flew away!"

Jupiter blinked at the girl. "She flew—?"

"Come on, Winnie," Pete interrupted, "don't tell stories. You wouldn't want my dad to get mad at us."

"No," the small girl said doubtfully, and began to sob. "I'll never get Anastasia back!"

"Gee, don't cry, Winnie," Bob said. "You'll find—"

Jupiter was frowning. "What do you mean about Anastasia *flying* away?"

"She did!" Winifred said, brushing away her tears. "I left her in her bed in the yard last night, and when I was going to bed, I looked out the window and saw her fly right up into a tree! My daddy looked for her up there this morning, and she's gone! She'll never come home!"

"Well," Jupiter said, "maybe we could take a look."

Pete groaned. "We've got to take the projector, Jupe."

"Dolls don't just fly, First," Bob pointed out.

"No, they don't," Jupiter acknowledged. The stocky First Investigator of the trio looked thoughtful. "And that's precisely why we're going to have a look at that tree. It won't take long."

Winifred dried her tears and smiled eagerly. "I'll show you!"

The boys followed her through the hedge and into the yard next door. The tree was an old avocado that grew near the street, beyond the fence that ran across the front of the property. Thick branches hung low over the Daltons' yard. Winifred pointed to the ground under a long branch.

"Anastasia was sleeping right there!"

The boys searched among the thick leaves and dangling green fruit of the old tree. They kicked through the layers of leaves on the ground under it.

"No doll in this tree," Pete declared.

"Nothing on the ground," Bob reported.

Jupiter walked around the fence to the street. There he could see that the avocado tree grew out of a narrow flower bed in front of the fence. He walked closer and studied the soft ground in the bed.

"Fellows!" the stout leader called out.

Skirting the tree branches, Bob and Pete went to the fence and looked over. Jupiter was pointing down. There, at the base of the tree, were four clear footprints in the flower bed. They looked like sneaker footprints, small and narrow.

"I'd say," Jupiter observed slowly, "that someone climbed this tree recently. Someone small and wearing sneakers."

"Sounds like a kid," Pete said. "Lots of kids climb the trees around here, Jupe."

"That's true," Jupiter agreed. "But it's also possible that someone climbed the tree, crawled out on one of those low branches over the yard, and reached down to grab the doll from the ground!"

"Gosh!" Bob said. "In the dark, that sure would look like the doll just flew up into the tree!"

"But," Pete wondered, "why would anyone want to swipe a kid's doll?"

Jupe shrugged and walked back around the fence. Just then a red-headed woman came out of the Daltons' house. She looked like Winifred, except bigger.

"Winnie? Peter? What are you doing?"

"Finding Anastasia, Mom," Winnie called. "They're detectives."

Mrs. Dalton smiled as she came forward. "Of course. I'd forgotten." Then she shook her head. "But I'm afraid Anastasia is gone, boys."

"You're sure the doll was stolen, Mrs. Dalton?" Bob said.

"I wasn't at first," Mrs. Dalton said, "but Winnie's father looked everywhere in the house and yard, and then we talked to the police."

"What did the police say?" asked Jupiter.

"They were very angry. It seems that there was a rash of thefts on this block last night."

"Other dolls were stolen?" Jupiter exclaimed.

"No. No more dolls, but a drill set, some tools, a microscope, and a few more items I forget. Nothing of any great value. Chief Reynolds is sure it's the work of juvenile vandals."

"Some dumb kids think it's so daring to steal," Pete said.

"Until they get caught!" Bob added.

Jupiter seemed disappointed. "I guess it does sound like kids stealing for kicks."

Winnie suddenly began to cry again. "I want Anastasia!"

"Gee," Pete said, glancing at his chums, "I guess we could try to find her. We know most of the local kids."

"That would be nice of you, boys," Mrs. Dalton said. "The police are too busy to do much about small thefts."

"But I have to hire them, Mom. Like on TV," Winnie cried, holding out her fifty cents. "Here."

Jupiter took the money solemnly. "You're our client now, Winnie. You stay home here and wait for our reports. All right?"

The small girl nodded happily, and the boys headed back to Pete's yard. They discussed where to begin their search and, by the time they reached Pete's driveway, decided to start by asking among their schoolmates if any kids had been acting funny. Suddenly they heard Pete's mother yelling behind the house:

"Get out of my garden! You! What are you doing?"

"Come on!" Pete cried.

The Investigators raced around behind the house just in time to see a strange figure with great black wings fly over the back fence and vanish! They stared. Pete's mother stood near her garden.

"Just look at my mums!" she cried. "He trampled them all!"

But the boys weren't looking at the ruined flowers. They were still staring at the fence where the figure had disappeared—a figure whose "wings" had been a black cape, and whose skinny face, looking back, had shown a thick mustache!

"Wow," Pete said, "that sure wasn't any kid!"

Jupiter turned and ran back to the garage. The other two boys ran after him. Jupiter pointed to where Mr. Crenshaw's movie projector had stood in its case.

"The projector," Jupiter said. "It's gone!"

2

One Mystery Solved

"So," Jupiter said, "no one can think of why a thief would want Pete's father's projector, Winnie's doll, and all the other stolen things." The stout leader paused dramatically. "Then maybe he *doesn't* want them!"

Pete and Bob both gaped at the First Investigator.

"Then why did—" Bob began.

"—he steal them?" Pete finished.

Hours had passed since the small man in the cape had escaped with Mr. Crenshaw's movie projector. The Three Investigators were meeting after dinner in their secret headquarters, an old mobile home trailer hidden under mounds of junk in a corner of The Jones Salvage Yard. Crammed with furniture, files, and homemade detective equipment, the trailer made an efficient base of operations—and a very private one. Jupiter's Uncle Titus and Aunt Mathilda, who owned the salvage yard, had long forgotten that the trailer was there. Secret entrances led into it, and a periscope let the boys see out of it. The boys were now gathered inside Headquarters to puzzle over the series of petty thefts on Pete's block.

Only one thing was sure—the thefts were not the work of kids. After the man in the cape had vanished that morning, the Investigators had found his footprints in Mrs. Crenshaw's garden. The footprints were exactly the same as those under Winnie Dalton's avocado tree! But why had the man stolen both a doll and a movie projector?

"Maybe," Pete said, "that man is a . . . a . . . you know —someone who steals things because he can't help stealing."

"A kleptomaniac," Bob said.

"That could be," Jupiter conceded, "but I don't think so. A kleptomaniac doesn't usually sneak around stealing from houses. He grabs things in stores and other public places."

"He's not a kleptomaniac, and he doesn't want what he's stealing," Bob said. "Then what's he doing?"

"I think," Jupiter said, "he's *looking* for something!"

Bob and Pete stared at the First Investigator. Confusion and doubt were all over their faces. Bob objected first.

"But, Jupe," the Records man of the team said slowly, "if he's after something, why steal so many different things? I mean, he must know what he wants, and if it's not anything he's taken, why did he take them?"

"He could have lousy eyesight," Pete suggested.

Bob groaned at the tall Second Investigator. Pete brought more muscle power than brain power to the group. "He'd have to be blind to mistake a doll and a movie projector for each other!" Bob pointed out.

"Okay," Pete said, "it's not the things, it's something hidden inside them! He knows it's hidden, but not exactly where!"

"As in our Crooked Cat Case." Jupiter nodded. "But that still leaves the same puzzle—assuming the thief knows what he's doing, then there must be something the same about all the things he's stolen. *They all must have something in common!*"

"A movie projector and a doll?" asked Bob in disbelief.

"There must be something," insisted Jupiter. "Some pattern to everything that was stolen. All we have to do is find it."

"Is that all, Jupe?" said Pete. "Winnie's doll, my dad's projector, and all the stuff on the list the police gave you when you called?" He picked the list from Jupiter's desk. "An electric drill kit, a microscope, a barometer, a wood-carving set, and a stone-polishing kit. All swiped on my block."

As Pete finished reading the list, the three junior detectives looked hopefully at each other. None of them spoke for some time.

"Well," Pete said at last, "they're not all electrical."

"And they're not all instruments," Bob said.

"Nor all toys," Jupiter added. "Or owned by kids." He pondered. "Maybe all were bought in the same place?"

Bob shook his head. "Not a barometer and a doll."

"And my dad bought his projector years ago in New York." Pete sighed. "Gee, Jupe, I don't see anything."

"There *must* be something alike about all of them,"

Jupiter insisted again. "Something simple. Think, fellows!"

"They're all solid," Pete offered. "I mean, no liquids."

"That's a big help!" declared Bob.

"No, Records, we have to try everything," Jupiter said. "All right, they're all solid objects. Are they all metal? No. All the same color? No. All—"

"They're all small enough to carry," Bob interrupted.

Jupiter leaped to his feet, his eyes alight. "Carry? That could be it! Come on, we have to talk to Winnie Dalton."

Jupiter was already raising the trap door in the floor of Headquarters. His fellow Investigators knew better than to ask him what he had in mind. Jupe never stopped for explanations when he was hot on a scent. Pete and Bob followed him through the trap door into Tunnel Two, a big, long pipe that led under the trailer and mounds of junk to Jupiter's outdoor workshop. There the boys grabbed their bikes and set off through the dusk for Pete's block. Jupe led the way, riding straight past Pete's yard and up the drive of the Daltons' house next door. Mrs. Dalton answered his ring, with Winifred in pajamas beside her.

"You found Anastasia!" the little girl cried.

"No, not yet." Jupiter shook his head. "Winnie, you said that Anastasia was *in her bed* when she flew up into the avocado tree. What kind of *bed?*"

"Her own bed," Winnie said. "She always—"

"Yes," Jupiter said impatiently, "but what was the bed like? I mean, it wasn't exactly a real bed, was it?"

Mrs. Dalton said, "No, it wasn't, Jupiter. My husband made it for Winnie from an old carrying case he had."

"A black case?" Jupiter said. "Twenty or so inches high?

Like a small trunk with a handle on top?"

"The same as my dad's projector case!" Pete exclaimed.

"Why, yes, boys," Mrs. Dalton said. "Just like that."

"Thanks." Jupiter's eyes blazed. "We'll be back, Winnie."

The Investigators rode their bikes around to Pete's yard and up into his garage. There was just enough light left to see by.

"Carrying cases!" Bob exulted. "All the stolen stuff must be in black carrying cases, just like Mr. Crenshaw's projector is!"

"Yes, Records," Jupiter said smugly. "That's the only thing that Winnie's doll could have in common with the other stolen items. Our thief must be looking for something in a black carrying case!"

"Gosh," Pete said, "but what, First?"

"Well, not a—" Jupiter began.

A noise came from behind the garage!

A sharp sound like something hitting wood, a muffled sound like an angry growl, and then the sound of something moving! The boys ran to the single rear window. Outside in the twilight a shape vanished into the thick bushes of Pete's backyard.

"The thief!" Pete exclaimed.

They went out the front of the garage and slipped cautiously around to the rear in the growing darkness. But nothing moved now, and there was no sound. Pete bent down under the rear garage window. He picked up a small object and stared at it.

"It's . . . it's . . . an animal's paw!" Pete stammered.

Jupiter took the paw. "A wolf's paw, I'd say—and very

old. It could be some kind of amulet, I think. Perhaps a lucky charm."

"It was right under the garage window," Pete said. "Someone was watching us, fellows! Listening! He heard us!"

"The thief in the cape, I'll bet," Bob decided.

Jupiter shook his head. "No, Records, this man was too tall. Perhaps there's more than one person after a black case—and whatever's in it."

"And now one of them knows that *we* know what he's after," Pete pointed out grimly.

"Yes," Jupiter agreed. His eyes gleamed in the dusk. "He knows, and that's how we'll catch him! We'll make him come to us!"

"How can we make him—" Pete began, dubious.

"He'll probably keep an eye on this block, and on us, Pete," Jupiter explained. "So we'll go around as if we're looking for the black case—and we'll find it! We'll act excited, as if we're sure we've found the right case, and—"

"A trap!" Bob and Pete exclaimed together.

Jupiter grinned in the fading twilight. "Yes, a little trap for our thief—or thieves!"

3

The Trap Is Sprung!

A thin fog rolled up from the harbor and the dark Pacific Ocean that night. The Rocky Beach street was silent. Two solitary street lamps shone eerily in the mist.

Somewhere a dog barked.

A cat darted quickly across the empty street.

For a time nothing else moved in the night.

Then Pete appeared in the open doorway of the lighted Crenshaw garage. The tall Second Investigator paced up and down, watching the dimly lit street as if waiting for something. From time to time he glanced behind him at several small black cases. They had been gathered earlier by the team and were clearly visible to anyone watching.

Suddenly, from a driveway up the block, Jupiter and Bob came running out. They carried another small black case and were clearly excited as they hurried along the misty street to Pete's house.

"What's up, fellows?" Pete called out.

Bob and Jupiter ran into the Crenshaw driveway.

"Jupe thinks we've found it!" Bob cried.

"Wait until you see what it is!" Jupiter echoed, panting up the driveway.

Inside the open doors of the garage, the three boys gathered eagerly around the small black case that Jupiter set down. The stocky leader of the trio opened the case and looked up at Pete with excited eyes. Pete stared down into the open case.

"Wow!" the tall boy said loudly. "That's something else!"

Jupiter raised his voice. "I'm certain it's what the thief has been looking for."

"Me, too," Bob agreed. "What'll we do with it, Jupe?"

"Well . . ." Jupiter seemed to ponder. "It's pretty late now. I should have been home an hour ago. We'd better lock it up here in the garage and take it to the police in the morning."

"It is late," Pete agreed.

"I have to get home, too," Bob admitted. "We can take it to the police early tomorrow."

They set the black case on the workbench in a corner, turned off the light, and went out, locking the garage doors with a padlock. Bob and Jupiter got on their bikes and, with a wave to Pete, rode off down the block and out of sight around the corner. Alone, Pete went into his house.

The dark, misty street became silent once more.

But around the corner, out of sight of anyone who might be watching the Crenshaw house and garage, Bob and

Jupiter quickly parked their bikes in the shadows of a thick grove of eucalyptus trees. Silently the boys began to slip through the dark rear yards of the houses on Pete's block. They reached the yard of the Dalton house next door to the Crenshaws, crept across it, and lay in the shadow of the high hedge that separated the Dalton yard from Pete's driveway.

The front door of the garage, dark now, was just beyond the hedge.

Carefully, the two Investigators wormed their way forward under the hedge. They lay where they were hidden, but where they could leap out onto Pete's driveway in an instant. At his bedroom window, which faced the garage, Pete was buttoning his pajamas in clear view. For a moment the Second Investigator stood in front of the window and yawned a few times. Then the light went out in his room.

In the misty night nothing moved.

Half an hour passed. Under the hedge, Jupiter's left leg began to go to sleep, and Bob battled to keep his teeth from chattering in the chill fog. A stray cat made a clatter among the garbage cans in the Dalton yard. Two men passed by on the street, talking loudly, but they didn't stop. Their voices faded away into the next block.

Jupiter began to think his plan wouldn't work. There was no sign of a thief. And Pete's parents, who were away for the evening, might come back too soon and spoil the trap.

Bob continued to shiver in the cold fog. Jupiter's eyes drooped in a doze. Then it happened!

"Jupe!" Bob whispered.

A man had appeared at the foot of the driveway, dimly

illuminated by the streetlight. It was the mustached thief in the cape!

"I see him," Jupiter whispered back.

The little man looked around nervously in the night, then started up the driveway toward the garage. Jupiter spoke low:

"Remember, first we let him break in, and then we jam the doors from outside! You guard the back window, I guard the doors, and Pete calls the police!"

Bob nodded quickly. The two boys watched tensely as the small thief took some kind of tool from a pocket in his wide cape and opened the garage-door padlock. He vanished inside the garage. Jupiter scrambled up.

"Now, Records! Hurry!"

They crawled out of the hedge, jumped up—and a brilliant shaft of light struck them directly in their eyes!

"What—!" Bob cried.

Almost blinded, they covered their eyes against the dazzling beam of light. It came from the side of the garage nearest the hedge.

Then the light was gone, and an eerie noise seemed to fill the night—a loud, chilling noise like the savage snarl of some wild beast!

The sound seemed to come from the same place where the dazzling light had been. As the frightened boys looked between the garage and the hedge, a face suddenly appeared, bathed in a ghostly glow of light.

A face—but not human! An animal face, broad and shaggy with black hair, its slitted eyes glowing red and its enormous mouth wide and jagged with sharp teeth! Long horns spread out from the massive head, and a long tail of hair grew up out of the top! A barbaric face, the savage teeth glowing like fire in the circle of light!

"Ju . . . Ju . . . Jupe!" Bob quavered.

Paralyzed, the two boys stared at the demonic face—and then the glow of light went out, and the face was gone!

Shivering, the boys stood there unable to move.

"Jupe! Bob!"

Pete was calling from the house. The Second Investigator stood at his bedroom window and pointed frantically down the driveway.

"He's got the case!" he yelled. "He's getting away!"

The small thief had slipped out of the garage and past Jupe and Bob while they stood frozen in fear. Now he was running out of the driveway and into the street, with his cape flying out behind him. He carried the black case that the boys had left in the garage as bait for their trap.

Bob was the first to recover. "Jupe, let's get him!"

He raced down the driveway with Jupiter behind him, and Pete joined them as they reached the street. The Second Investigator pointed down the block. The caped thief was running toward a red Datsun parked across the street. The three boys pursued—and Bob hurtled heavily into a man who appeared directly in their path.

"What's going on here?" the newcomer demanded in a sharp voice, grabbing hold of Bob. "Don't you boys know better than to run into people?"

He was a slender gray-haired man, wearing rimless glasses on a black ribbon attached to the vest of his prim gray suit. His left eye twitched nervously as he peered at the boys like a suspicious schoolteacher.

"That man's a thief!" Bob cried, pointing to the man in the cape who was getting into the red Datsun.

"And he's getting away!" Pete groaned.

Down the street the Datsun started and roared away. The boys and the thin stranger watched it vanish.

"A thief is a serious matter, young man," the stranger said severely. "Just what did he steal?"

"A black carrying case!" Bob said hotly. "And if you hadn't stopped us, we—"

"And what was in the case?" the man asked.

"I– in—?" Pete stammered.

Jupiter said quickly, "We can't say what was in it, sir."

"I see." The man glared. "Some juvenile game, eh? Well, I suggest you boys go home and stop such antics!"

He turned and walked stiffly away. Jupiter stared thoughtfully after the man until he turned the corner and was gone.

"Does that man live here on your block, Pete?" he asked.

"I never saw him before," Pete said. "Hey! You think he stopped us to let that thief get away?"

Jupiter nodded slowly. "I think it's possible, Second."

"Jupe?" Bob said. "What about that . . . face we saw? It helped the thief, too. What was it?"

Jupiter shook his head. "I don't know, Records."

"What face?" Pete asked.

Bob described the eerie face he and Jupiter had seen. Pete's view of it from the house had been blocked by the garage.

"Ulp." Pete swallowed. "Maybe it was just the fog."

"Whatever it was," Bob said grimly, "the thief's escaped!"

"Perhaps not yet," Jupiter said, and grinned at his two companions. "Just in case something went wrong, I took the precaution of putting one of our 'homer' signals in the black case! With any luck, fellows, it'll lead us right to our thief."

"If he isn't too far away already," Pete moaned.

"I don't think he is," Jupiter said. "He's been around this block for two days, so he's probably staying somewhere nearby. Let's find out."

Jupe took out one of the sender-receiver signal sets he'd built for the Investigators, and switched it onto "receive." For a moment, there was nothing. Then it began—a steady, slow *beep . . . beep . . . beep . . .*

"There!" Jupiter crowed. "Maybe two miles away!"

They ran for their bikes.

4

The Demon Attacks!

The steady *beep . . . beep . . . beep . . .* led the boys through the night toward the Pacific Ocean. They rode their bikes slowly in the thin fog, listening to the beeps and watching the arrow on Jupiter's receiver dial.

"We're getting closer," Jupiter said. "It looks as if he's near the harbor, but along the beach a way."

When used as a receiver, Jupiter's directional signal device worked two ways: the beeps got louder and faster as the receiver got closer to the sender unit, and a simple arrow-pointer on a dial showed if the signal was coming from right, left, or straight ahead. There was also a built-in emergency signal—a red light that flashed on one set when anyone said the word "help" near another set—but that didn't interest the boys now.

"The beeps are getting a little stronger," Pete said as they reached the beachfront.

"The arrow's pointing left," Bob added as he peered at the dial in Jupiter's bike basket.

The direction was away from the harbor. The boys turned down the coast road, which was all but deserted in the misty night. Traffic was sparse, and the usual beach strollers and teen-age party goers were not out in the cold fog. The boys pedaled in silence except for the beeping, which grew steadily louder and faster.

They were passing through an area of motels when the beeping suddenly began to get lower and slower again!

"We've passed it!" Bob exclaimed.

"He must be in one of those motels," Pete said.

"I'm sure of it," Jupiter decided. "We'd better leave the bikes somewhere, and move in on foot. Careful now. Remember, he knows who we are."

The Investigators hid their bikes in a group of ornamental bushes planted between two motels, and started walking back along the dark road. The beeping of Jupiter's homing receiver grew louder again, and faster, until the needle arrow on the dial pointed directly away from the road toward the beach.

"He must be in there!" Jupiter said.

He pointed to a motel shrouded in the mist between the road and the beach. A pink-and-green neon sign flashed the name Palm Court on and off, and colored spotlights lit up the front of the motel. It was a small, one-story affair, built in three sections that were placed in a U-shape facing the road. Cars were parked in front of most of the units. From the road the boys studied the cars in the courtyard. Pete finally shook his head.

"Gosh, Jupe," he said. "I don't see the red Datsun!"

The red car wasn't there.

"You think he found the homer?" Bob said. "Left it around here to fool us?"

"I guess he could have," Jupiter said uneasily.

"He sure knows by now we tricked him," Pete pointed out. "He's had plenty of time to open that case and find nothing in it but an old iron pipe!"

"Yes, I guess he knows it was a trap," Jupiter agreed unhappily. Then his voice grew firm again. "But let's not give up until we know we're beaten! We'll find just where our homer signal is coming from."

Without waiting for the others to agree, the stout investigator began to trot through the foggy night. Eyes fixed on his receiver, he circled around behind the buildings with Bob and Pete following. The motel backed directly onto the wide beach. The boys worked their way silently through the darkness between the rear of the motel and the dunes and tall palms wreathed in swirling mist.

Halfway along the rear section, the needle on the dial pointed directly at one unit!

"It's dark, Jupe!" Bob whispered. "No one's in it!"

"He's gone!" Peter groaned.

"Perhaps he had to go somewhere, and is coming back, and maybe he didn't even open the case!" Jupiter exclaimed. "Come on!"

Bent low, the First Investigator began to cautiously approach the rear of the dark motel unit. Pete and Bob followed, their feet making a soft crunching sound in the coarse, pebbly beach sand. The needle on the directional signal pointed straight at the motel unit, and the beeping grew faster, and faster, and . . .

"Down!" Pete ordered, pushing Bob and Jupiter down on the sand and falling flat himself.

The back door of the darkened unit was opening!

A slim figure stepped out into the night and stood motionless for a moment, looking all around in the dark mist. His face was hidden by the shadows close to the motel. The boys held their breath where they lay in the open, covered only by the drifting fog, and tried to sink deeper into the sand.

The faceless man seemed to stiffen and search the night more carefully, as if he'd heard or seen something.

The beeps! thought Jupiter in alarm. His hand was pressing the receiver into the sand, but the beeps were not entirely muffled. He felt wildly for the "off" button and pushed it. The faint beeping vanished. Slowly Jupiter let out his breath.

Close to the motel, the shadowy man listened for another moment, seemed to hear nothing suspicious any more, and walked away around the corner of the building. As he turned the corner, he passed through the dim light coming from the corner unit.

"Jupe!" Bob whispered.

It was the man in the prim gray suit who had stopped them from chasing the caped thief on Pete's block!

"He *is* mixed up with the thief!" Pete exclaimed quietly.

"So it would appear," Jupiter whispered back.

The boys remained flat on the sand for a few more minutes. The thin man didn't return, so they slipped around the corner after him. Spying no one, they crept forward to the break between the rear and side sections of the motel. Through it they could see the man across the courtyard, getting into a gleaming black Mercedes in front of the motel office. The elegant car drove away.

The boys went back to the dark unit and peered in between the partly closed drapes of the rear window. The room was faintly lit by the colored spotlights in the motel courtyard, shining through the drapes of the front window. No one seemed to be inside—but there were dark shapes on the floor.

"Aha!" said Jupe softly. He tried the back door and it opened. Pete and Bob followed him inside.

"Watch the front, Second," Jupiter said.

Small black cases stood on the floor all through the dark room. While Pete took up his post at the front window, Bob and Jupiter checked the cases.

"It's all here!" Bob said. "Everything that was stolen."

"Yes," Jupiter agreed, "including Winnie's doll and our iron pipe! And we still have no idea what the thief was looking for. Bob, you take the left, I'll take the right, and search for clues that might tell us what the thief is really after."

But the motel room was almost bare, with no suitcases or clothes or anything else that might reveal the thief's intentions.

Pete spoke from the front window. "A red car just turned in!" He peered intently through a crack in the drapes. "It's the Datsun, and it's coming here!"

"Let's go outside and watch what he does!" Jupiter said.

They hurried out the back and crouched down just outside the rear window. Moments later the lights went on, and the

Investigators saw the small thief clearly for the first time. He was very short, not much more than five feet tall, and wore a shabby, patched sport jacket and wrinkled brown pants under the voluminous cape. His hair was gray and rumpled as if he never combed it, his face was thin and narrow with small teeth and a sharp nose, and his eyes were small and watery. He looked like some small wizened mouse behind his thick mustache.

"Wow," Pete whispered at the window, "he doesn't look like much of a thief."

"Not a very good one anyway," Bob said. "Look how nervous he is, Jupe! A scared rat."

The little thief stood just inside the open motel room door, staring toward the black cases on the floor. Something seemed to be bothering him. He frowned, repeatedly wriggling his pointy nose like a mouse testing the air for dangerous scents. The boys saw his lips moving as if he were talking to himself. Jupiter nudged his two companions.

"I think he knows someone's been in the room!" he whispered urgently.

"Then let's get out of here!" Pete answered.

Staying low, they crawled away from the window to the cover of the first sand dune. Streamers of fog still swirled in the air. The rows of tall palms along the beach stood like ghostly sentinels. Behind the dune, the boys held a quick conference.

"Maybe we should capture him," Bob suggested. "He's pretty small. The three of us ought to be able to grab him."

Jupiter disagreed. "No, Records, that's asking for trouble. Trapping him in a garage is one thing. Physically grabbing him is another. He could be armed and desperate!"

"But we have to do something," Pete urged.

"I guess it's time to call the police," Jupiter decided. "Pete can stay and watch. Bob, you circle around and get the license number of the Datsun in case he leaves. I'll find a telephone and call Chief Reynolds. Then I'll come—"

A flash of light cut him short! Light, and a puff of thick white smoke on a dune near them, and a savage sound:

"*Ahhhhhhhhrrrrrrrrrrrrr—!*"

A barbaric figure stood on top of the dune.

"The . . . the . . . face . . . !" Bob stammered.

Shaggy, with long horns, blazing red slit-eyes, and rows of jagged teeth that glowed like fire, it was the wild face Bob and Jupiter had seen at the garage! But now they saw the whole figure—a tall demonic shape with hair and fur hanging from thick, padded arms and legs. Bones hung around its neck. Bones, bells, rattles, and stalks of grain protruded from a belt around its waist. And draped over its chest and back was the skin of a wolf. The wolf head seemed to snarl straight at the boys!

"Wha . . . what . . . is . . . it?" Pete quavered.

Before Bob or Jupiter could answer, the barbarous, eerily lit figure began to dance in the night. The bells, rattles, and bones on it jangled and rasped. Slowly and ponderously, the creature danced straight toward the boys!

"Run, guys!" yelled Bob.

5 ━━━━━━━━━━━━━━━━━━━━━━━

Panic and More Panic

The Three Investigators fled wildly across the dark beach, panting and stumbling in the pebbly sand.

"Run for those rocks!" Pete yelled.

To their right, a high bank of rocks crossed the beach from the dunes and extended down into the ocean to form a small breakwater. The Three Investigators raced for the bank's cover. As they reached the base of the rocks, they looked back.

"It . . . it's gone!" Bob said shakily, unbelieving.

The beach stretched dark and empty behind them. Nothing moved in the night except a few cars that passed on the distant coast road, their headlights dimmed by the mist.

"It . . . was . . . there," Pete gasped. "Wasn't it?"

"We saw it! We heard it!" Bob cried.

"Yes," said Jupiter as he collapsed onto a rock, trying to

29

get his breath after the hard running. "We saw it, and we heard it, but . . . what did we really see and hear, fellows?"

Pete and Bob sank onto the sand.

"Oh, no!" Pete moaned. "Not a ghost! Say it was real, Jupe!" The Second Investigator gulped. "No, don't! What am I saying!"

"I don't think it was a ghost, Second," said Jupiter uneasily, still puffing. "While there may be some psychic phenomena we call ghosts, this one—"

"Some kind of trick, Jupe?" Bob suggested. "An illusion?"

"How could an illusion dance right at us?" Pete said.

Jupiter pondered. "I don't know."

"It looked like some kind of demon," said Bob. "A demon that's half animal, half human."

"You mean it's a devil?" asked Pete in alarm. "A real live devil?"

"It did bear some resemblance to a tribal devil figure," admitted Jupiter. "Hmmm. Well, whatever it was, it was meant to scare us off, that's certain."

"But we won't let it scare us off, will we, Jupe!" Bob said stoutly.

"I will!" Pete decided. "Far off!"

Jupiter and Bob smiled in the dark. They both knew that such talk was just Pete's way of relieving tension. When the time came for action, it was usually Pete who was in front.

The Investigators sat by the rocks for a while, getting back their wind. Now and then Pete peered uneasily into the fog, as if expecting to see the demon figure coming at him again. But nothing happened.

"All right, time to get organized," announced Jupe. "I

suggest we go out to the road and circle back to the motel. We'll go on with the plan just as it was. Only while I call the police, fellows, you two had better look for a second man around that room. I'm convinced now that there must be at least two thieves. Remember how that little man in the cape seemed to be talking to himself in the room? I don't think he was—I think he was talking to someone behind him, outside the front door where we couldn't see him."

"Maybe he was talking to that thing we saw," Bob said.

"Oh, swell!" Pete moaned. "A trained *thing!* Just what we need."

"Don't worry, Pete." Bob laughed. "Trained *thing,* or an illusion, it's gone now."

"Oh, no, it's not!" cried Pete. "Look!"

The boys froze!

"Ahhhhhhrrrrrrrrrrrrrrr—!"

High on the rocks, directly above them, the demon figure had reappeared. The massive, shaggy, horned head, the glowing red-slit eyes and luminous rows of teeth, and the dangling wolf head on its chest transfixed the shaking boys. Even as they stared, the monster began to dance and caper. The clicking and jangling of its bones and bells sent terror into the night. Suddenly the shaggy apparition boomed out in an eerie, hollow voice that seemed to come from everywhere:

"All who defile the spirits are destroyed!"

The voice broke the spell that held the boys fast. In panic, they scrambled up and turned to flee down the dark beach. But as Bob turned, his foot struck a heavy rock buried in the sand, and he sprawled flat on the beach, the wind knocked out of him.

Running, Pete and Jupiter heard the thud of Bob's body. They stopped and looked back in horror at their fallen comrade!

On the rocks, the barbarous apparition gave a savage laugh and bent forward to leap down on the helpless boy.

"Be warned, defilers!"

Pete bent down, picked a rock from the sand, and hurled it with all his strength directly at the apparition.

"Ahhhhrrrr—!"

The savage shape stepped backward, shook its massive head, then crouched once more to spring.

"Throw, Jupe!" Pete shouted, and hurled another stone.

Jupiter grabbed a stone and threw it. Again and again the two boys hurled missiles at the monster as Bob struggled to his feet.

"Fools! Be warned!"

A flash of light, a cloud of white smoke—and the demon figure was gone!

"Ulp!" Pete swallowed hard.

Bob came panting up to them. "Thanks, fellows! For a minute—"

"It's gone!" Pete said. "Just like that!"

"Let's take a look!" Jupiter said grimly.

Reluctantly, Pete and Bob followed him up onto the rocks. They looked in all directions. Nothing moved on the sand, or rocks, or anywhere. The apparition had dissolved into the mist once more. Jupiter bent down.

"Ashes!" He touched a mound of whitish ash. "Hot ashes!"

The small pile of hot ash was all that remained of the savage figure.

"Let . . . let's go home," Pete said.

"Not yet!" Jupiter said stubbornly. "We'll do just as we said!"

"Oh no," Pete groaned. "You mean—back to the motel?"

"Yes, Second. And I'll call Chief Reynolds."

The police came ten minutes after Jupiter called. But it was too late! When Pete and Bob returned to the motel, they found that the red Datsun was gone, the small thief had checked out, and the room had nothing left in it except the stolen black cases.

"The manager says that your little man was alone, and left no forwarding address," Chief Reynolds reported. "He undoubtedly used a false name and false identification, boys. But we're looking for his Datsun. He's probably a long way off by now, but we'll find him. And we won't be put off by any demon illusion trick!"

Jupiter smiled politely as the Chief chuckled.

"Well, boys," Chief Reynolds went on, "you've done fine work. All the stolen items are here, and we'll see that they get back to the owners. Congratulations! Another case solved, eh? Come on, I'll drive you home."

"Thank you, sir," Jupiter said. "But we have our bikes here. We'll ride home."

The Investigators retrieved Mr. Crenshaw's movie projector and their black case with the homer in it, then picked up their bikes. They pedaled to the salvage yard in silence. But as Pete and Bob prepared to ride on to their houses, their portly leader spoke:

"We'll meet first thing tomorrow, fellows. This case isn't solved until the police find that thief. Perhaps they'll have some word by morning. And then, perhaps, we can find out something about that demon figure. I'm sure it was no illusion!"

"N . . . not an . . . illusion?" Pete's voice quavered.

"When you hit it with that rock, it cried out and staggered back, Second. Illusions don't cry out."

"You mean it's—real?" Bob said.

"I'm certain it's real, Records," Jupiter said. "But perhaps not human!"

6

Jupe Makes Deductions

"This case is a long way from over!" Jupiter announced. "In fact, fellows, I think it's barely begun!"

The trio of junior detectives were in their hidden trailer headquarters the next morning. After hurried breakfasts, Bob and Pete had biked over to the salvage yard and found Jupiter in their office busily writing on a large note pad at the desk.

"Gosh, Jupe, didn't the police find the thief?" asked Pete.

"No, they did not," answered Jupiter. "But they found his Datsun—abandoned in the center of town. I spoke to Chief Reynolds just a few minutes ago. He said the car is a dead end. It was rented—under an assumed name. The chief is convinced that the thief has left town. But I'm not! In fact, I'm sure he's somewhere close by!"

"How do you figure that?" demanded Bob.

35

"I don't think the man has yet found what he's looking for. Remember, everything reported stolen was left in that motel room," Jupiter reminded him. "Besides, if the thief had found what he's after, he wouldn't have tried so hard to scare us off!"

"But maybe he found it last night after he skipped the motel," Bob said.

"Possible, Records, but not likely. Chief Reynolds told me no new thefts had been reported on Pete's block. I think we can safely assume the thief is still searching."

"Then where is what he wants?" Pete wondered.

"That, Second, is what we must discover!"

"But how, Jupe?" Bob demanded.

"By logic and deduction," Jupiter declared a trifle smugly. "First, what do we *know* so far?"

"The thief wants something in a small black case!"

"He knows it is somewhere on Pete's block!"

"And," Jupiter said, "it doesn't *belong* to anyone on Pete's block."

Bob and Pete stared at him.

"Because while our thief must know *what* he wants, he clearly doesn't know *where* it is or who has it! If he knew *who* had it, he'd have stolen from only *one* place, but he stole black cases from all over the block!"

"But," Bob objected, "if he knows what it is, he has to know who it belongs to."

"Oh, he knows who it belongs to—it belongs to him!" Jupiter said. "At least, he had it last, I'm certain."

Pete only looked more confused, but Bob understood.

"You mean it's something he *lost!* Of course!"

"Exactly," Jupiter said. "Lost, or had stolen from him."

Bob thought hard. "He doesn't know who took it or found it, but somehow he knows it was someone on Pete's block."

Pete still seemed confused. "But, First, why doesn't he just *ask* for it? If it's his, why not just go door to door and ask who found it? Or tell the police if it was swiped?"

"Because, while he had it last, I don't think it really belongs to him!" Jupiter said triumphantly. "He's been hiding, sneaking around, grabbing cases, and trying to scare us off. The missing object must be something important, probably very valuable, and something he stole himself!"

"Wow!" Pete exclaimed. "He swiped it, and lost it!"

"Yes, that's exactly what I think happened!"

Bob frowned. "Gosh, First, I don't remember hearing about any important robbery in town."

"Possibly it didn't happen in Rocky Beach," Jupiter said, "or perhaps the theft hasn't been discovered yet. Our caped thief seems awfully anxious to find whatever it is fast."

"So we'd better find it faster!" Bob said excitedly. Then his face dropped like a deflated balloon. "But how? If *he* doesn't know who has it, how can *we* find out?"

"And, Jupe," Pete said slowly, "if the thief doesn't know who has whatever it is, how does he know it's someone on my block?"

"That," Jupiter said, "is the puzzle we must solve if we are to catch our culprit."

Bob and Pete looked at each other as if to say that their brainy chum had lost all sight of reality. This didn't disturb Jupiter at all. The stout First Investigator sat there grinning at them like the cat that's just swallowed a very tasty canary.

"Gosh, First," Bob said finally, missing Jupiter's mischievous grin. "How do we even know where to start?"

"We know," Jupiter said happily, "because I've already started!" He leaned forward. "When did the thefts begin?"

"Two nights ago," Pete said.

Jupiter nodded. "And I think our thief would have discovered his loss pretty quickly, and started looking. So he must have lost his black case a little earlier in the day. Say, in the late afternoon."

"Somewhere close to Pete's block?" Bob suggested.

"I think so, Records," Jupiter replied. "And how does someone lose a valuable case? Something he'd be careful with? Something he'd never forget under normal conditions?"

"By conditions not being normal!" Bob said.

"Yes," Jupiter said. "Some abnormal happening distracted him, perhaps scared him, and made him act too fast!"

"An enemy came after him?" Bob suggested. "That thin guy with the funny glasses?"

"The police scared him?" Pete offered.

"Or he was in a car accident," said Jupiter. "An accident that made him get out of the car with the case, and then jump back into the car without it and drive off fast to escape trouble."

"And leave the case behind!" Bob said. "But how will we ever—?"

Pete groaned. "He's tricked us, Records. He knows there *was* an accident. He's already checked with the police."

Jupiter grinned. "Yes, Second, I did. And at exactly five-thirty P.M. two days ago a car skidded off the street into a yard just around the corner from Pete's block! The driver drove away—hit and run. No one got the license number, but witnesses said the car was a red Datsun! I'm sure the driver was the thief and that he left the case behind. So we'll go and ask if—"

Suddenly, Pete raised his hand and listened. Far off outside the boys heard angry voices arguing.

"Look through the See-All," Bob exclaimed.

Pete raised their periscope made by Jupiter from a piece of old stovepipe, and peered through the eyepiece. He had a clear view over the mounds of junk that surrounded the trailer.

"It's your Aunt Mathilda, Jupe," Pete reported—and stiffened. "She's with that thin man who stopped us on my block, and who was in the motel room last night! He's walking away!"

"Hurry!" Jupiter urged.

They dropped through the trap door and crawled along Tunnel Two. Outside, they ran around the junk to where they could see Aunt Mathilda across the yard. She was looking after the thin man as he got into the same black Mercedes they'd seen at the Palm Court Motel. As the boys ran up, the car drove away.

Panting, Jupe asked, "Who was that, Aunt Mathilda? What did he want?"

"He was skulking around the yard," she snapped. "When I asked what he was doing, he wanted to know if anyone— like three young boys—had sold me anything in a black case." She fixed the boys with her sharp eyes. "He seemed angry. What have you scamps been up to now?"

"He's the one who's up to something!" Pete said hotly.

Jupiter explained about the black cases, their suspicions, and helping Chief Reynolds. "We're going to the accident scene right now, Aunt Mathilda. To try to trace the real case."

"Jupiter, I had some chores lined up for you today!"

Jupe's face fell. He looked so woeful that Aunt Mathilda relented.

"Oh well, if it's to help Chief Reynolds," she said.

The Investigators ran for their bikes.

7

An Answer to a Puzzle

The house was a white cottage only three doors from the corner of Pete's block. Set back from the street behind a white picket fence, it had a profuse rose garden and a neat lawn. But now the fence was smashed, four of the rose bushes had been torn up, and the lawn was half-ruined.

Jupiter rang the bell. The woman who answered had white hair and an angry face. She glared past the boys at her ruined yard, her face growing even angrier.

"What do you boys want?" she demanded irately. "I have enough trouble without children bothering me!"

"We're very sorry about your garden, ma'am," Jupiter said in his most elegant and polite voice. "We came—"

"Can you tell us who did it?" Pete blurted out.

"I have no time to be wasting on—" the woman began.

"Of course not, ma'am," Jupiter said, kicking Pete. "A

tragic loss. That fine Queen Elizabeth, and a Mister Lincoln, too."

"You grow roses, young man?" The woman was surprised.

"Not like yours, I'm afraid," Jupiter said.

She beamed. "I have won prizes, I must admit."

"And he just drove off?" Jupiter said, shaking his head as he looked toward the roses. "The man who did that?"

"The horrible little villain! Without a word!"

Jupiter said alertly, "A small man? In a cape, perhaps?"

"Why, yes, something like a cape. He jumped out of that red car as if he were afraid it would explode. Then he jumped back in and drove right off through my fence! Some of my neighbors tried to stop him, but he was gone. They didn't even see his license plate."

Jupiter's voice was casual. "I suppose he didn't leave anything behind to identify him? A suitcase?"

"Nothing I saw," the lady said sadly. "But I really didn't see very much. It happened so fast, and then so many people crowded into the yard."

"I'm sure they all meant well," Jupiter said. "Thank you, ma'am."

He motioned to Bob and Pete, and the three of them left the battered yard.

"It sounds like him, all right," Bob said.

"And he did get out of the car!" Pete pointed out.

"Yes," Jupiter said. "Perhaps a neighbor saw more."

In the next yard a man was out in the sunny morning watering his lawn. The boys walked up to him.

"Excuse me, sir," Jupiter said, "but could we ask you some questions about the accident next door? We're investigating—"

"Investigating?" The man looked at them suspiciously.

"For a school project," Bob said quickly. "We're studying hit-and-run drivers in social studies class."

Jupiter sometimes forgot that most adults didn't take them seriously as detectives, often refusing to even talk to them. But adults almost always approved of a school project! The man smiled at once.

"That's fine, we all need to learn respect for the law," he said. "But I'm afraid I can't help you much. I was in the house when I saw that car skid and smash the fence. It started steaming and the driver jumped out. Had a tool kit or something, probably thought the car was on fire. But it was only a broken water hose, easy to fix at any garage. By the time I got outside he was gone."

"A tool kit?" Pete exclaimed. "What did he do with it?"

"I wouldn't know. There was getting to be a crowd around by then, kids and all. Maybe Kastner across the street there saw more. He's usually on his porch."

They thanked the man, and crossed the street to a large blue house. An old man sat on the wide front porch.

"I know Mr. Kastner," Pete said as they approached. "From church. He's a deacon." As they reached the porch, Pete said, "Hello, Mr. Kastner. Could we talk to you about—"

"The accident over there, eh, Peter?" the old man broke in, his eyes twinkling. "I've been watching you. I'd say The Three Investigators are after that hit-and-run driver, right?"

"Yes, sir." Pete grinned. "Can you tell us anything?"

"Saw it all, my boy. What do you want to know?"

"The driver had a tool kit," Bob said. "Did you see it? Maybe he left it behind? A small black case?"

"As a matter of fact, he did! I told the detective—"

Jupiter's eyes narrowed. "Detective, sir?"

"Yep, came around maybe only five minutes after that Datsun drove off," Mr. Kastner said. "Real little guy with a pointy face and a ratty sport coat. They should pay the police more. Wanted to know if I'd seen a black case on the ground over there. Told him I sure had. Saw some boy on a bike pick it up. Just about your age, Peter, or a little older. Think I've seen him around here, but can't place him, you know?"

"What did he do with the case?" Bob asked eagerly.

"Rode off with it. Around onto Peter's street. Last I saw of him. He didn't come back out. Told the detective so, and he ran off to your block pretty excited." The old man frowned. "Funny, now that I think of it, but the detective was on foot. Hadn't a car."

"Thanks, Mr. Kastner!" Pete exclaimed.

The boys hurried off toward Pete's street.

"It was the thief, wasn't it, Jupe!" Bob said as they reached Pete's corner. "Pretending to be a detective!"

"He came back for the case!" Pete said.

"And Mr. Kastner told him about the boy on the bike," Jupiter said. "That's how he knew it had to be on Pete's block."

Bob stopped, his face dismayed. "But how could the thief be sure that kid *stayed* on this block? I mean, all Mr. Kastner said was that he saw the boy ride onto this street and not come back out. But he could have just ridden right on to the next block, or the one after that, couldn't he?"

Jupiter looked stunned. "There must be some—"

"The sewer!" Pete cried, looking up the street toward the far end of the block. "I forgot about the sewer work!"

A gaping excavation lay across the entire street near the end of the block, extending through the sidewalks and into the yards.

"Gosh," Bob realized. "No one could ride past that, even on a bicycle! So if the kid rode onto this block, and didn't ride back the way he'd come, he has to live here somewhere!"

"Pete," Jupiter said, "what boys our age live here?"

"Just the new kid, Joey Marsh. He lives four houses up from me," Pete said. "And that Frankie Bender. You know, Jupe, that bully who runs with the gang of dumb wise guys at school?"

"I remember him. Okay, let's find them."

Pete led them to a big house four doors beyond his home. A smiling matronly woman answered Pete's ring. He asked for Joey.

"You're Peter Crenshaw, aren't you?" Mrs. Marsh said. "I'm sure Joey will be sorry he missed you, but he's visiting his grandmother in San Francisco."

"When did he go up there, ma'am?" Pete asked.

"Almost a week ago, Peter."

They thanked her, and Pete took them across the street and on up the block to a bungalow on a shady lot.

"I guess that just leaves Frankie Bender," Pete said as they walked up the tree-lined driveway toward the house. "I sure hate to have to talk to him, but if anyone swiped the case, it'd be Frankie."

"We had better be careful what we say," Jupiter decided. "We don't want to make him suspicious—"

A shower of leaves suddenly cascaded down over them, and something whistled through the air above their heads!

"What—!" Bob cried out.

Another object zinged above them! Small and quick, singing past like a bullet, and tearing through the tree leaves overhead. And another, and . . .

"Owwwwwww!" Pete yelped as he was hit squarely on the leg.

"Down, guys!" Bob cried.

They fell down on the driveway as more projectiles buzzed above them.

8

The Black Case!

"Ha-ha-ha!"

The sneering laugh came from on top of the garage! A short, barrel-chested boy about Pete's age stood up on the roof where he had been hiding like a sniper. A wicked-looking slingshot dangled from his hand.

"Ping—ping—ping!" He laughed. "I could have picked you off one by one like rabbits! Don't you creeps even know enough to take cover? Boy, you don't know nothin'!"

Pete jumped up, furious. "You could have broken my leg with that, Bender! A slingshot's dangerous!"

"Aw, nuts," Frankie Bender said. He took something from a bag at his belt and shot it lazily at Pete. "See? Just wooden balls, that's all. Besides, I'm a sharpshooter, and I was just buzzin' you mostly. Look!"

Bender shot a ball full force. It whizzed just over Pete's

head. Pete paled, but stood his ground. Jupiter walked closer to the boy on the roof and looked up.

"You're stupid, Frank Bender," Jupiter said quietly. "Someday you'll hurt someone, and then you'll be in real trouble. Meanwhile, I believe there's a law against that kind of slingshot."

"Hey!" Bender grinned uneasily. "You talk so smart, don't you even know a joke?"

"You're the joke, Frankie, not your slingshot!" Pete said hotly.

Jupe continued calmly, "I intend to report you to the police."

Bender's grin faded, and he scowled down from the roof. "You better not, Fatso! What do you goody-goodies want here anyway? You're trespassing on my driveway. Yeh, that's it, you're trespassers! I was defending my property!"

"You better read some law!" Bob said, and then he laughed. "Boy, what you don't know, Frankie!"

"Don't try to be clever, Bender, it takes thinking," Jupiter said drily. "What we want is that black carrying case you stole from the accident two days ago. And what was in it."

"Hey, how do you—?" Bender stopped, his small eyes sly in his pudgy face. "What case? I mean, I don't know nothing about any black case."

"You were seen with it!" Pete retorted.

"Not me, no sir," Bender said.

"We've got witnesses!" Bob declared.

"Yeh? So why haven't the cops been around?"

"Because they don't yet know what we know," Jupiter said. "Listen, Bender—the man in that Datsun was a thief!

What's in that case is stolen property. You could get in trouble."

"I don't know what you're talking about," Bender said.

"Don't be dumb," Jupiter said, shaking his head. "If you don't get into trouble with the police, you will with the thief! He's looking hard for his case right now. If he finds you—!"

On the garage roof, Frankie Bender bit his lip for a moment. He looked nervous. Then his chin lifted stubbornly.

"Phooey! You're trying to trick me. I never saw any black case. Now get out of here before I whistle up my gang!"

"We'll call the police if we have to," Jupiter said.

"You don't scare me, Jupiter Jones! If you don't get out of here, maybe *I'll* call the cops. I'm telling you to leave!"

Pete said, "Come down here and tell us!"

"Without your gang," Bob challenged.

Bender reddened. "Beat it! Now!"

"We'd better go, fellows," Jupiter said.

Reluctantly, Bob and Pete followed Jupiter back down the driveway. Jupiter turned down the street toward Pete's house, where they had left their bikes.

"We're not giving up, are we, First?" Bob said. "I'm sure he's got the case!"

"He's got it all right," Pete said flatly.

"Yes, he has," Jupiter said, "and we have him worried. The moment he thinks we've really gone away, he'll go to wherever he has the case to make sure it's still there."

"You think he'll lead us to it?" Pete said as the boys crossed the street to his house.

Jupiter nodded. "He was pretty anxious to get rid of us, and he's nervous. He'll check to be sure he still has it, and when he does—we'll be there!"

The moment they were out of sight in Pete's backyard, the Investigators began to trot through the other backyards in the direction of the Bender house. They reached the house facing Bender's and reconnoitered. A line of thick bushes grew between this yard and the next. Like skirmishers on dangerous patrol in enemy country, the boys slipped through the shrubbery until they were almost at the sidewalk. Peeking out, they had a clear view of Frankie Bender's front yard across the street.

The boys crouched down and kept the Bender house under observation. A few minutes later, Frankie Bender came out of the garage and hurried down his driveway toward the street.

"Jupe," Bob whispered, "he's leaving!"

"He doesn't have any case!" Pete added.

"Then we'll follow him," Jupiter said. "Keep hidden!"

The oxlike bully, his slingshot stuck into his belt, walked to the unblocked end of the street, and turned away from the ocean. Moving out of sight from yard to yard, the shadowing trio followed him to the edge of town and out into the brown foothills of the dry mountains that surrounded Rocky Beach.

Bender looked nervously around from time to time, but, like most people, he didn't know how to observe and never saw the boys tailing him. He crossed the railroad tracks and went up the steep slope of a low mountain covered with thorny chapparal and studded with dull green, twisted live oaks. Halfway up, with the Investigators slipping from tree to bush below, he reached a thick growth of tangled mesquite —and vanished!

"He's gone!" Pete cried low.

"Careful," Jupiter warned, "he could be watching."

They worked their way up slowly, crawling the last few yards to the growth of heavy mesquite. Pete raised his head to peer through the dry bushes.

"It's a cave!" he whispered. "It opens behind the bushes."

They crawled through the tough mesquite, which tore at their clothes, and into the dark opening in the mountain. Still on their hands and knees, they crept along a short tunnel that suddenly opened up into a large, dim cave. For a time they looked around without getting up or moving.

Their quarry was nowhere in sight. But as their eyes became fully accustomed to the dim light, they saw chairs and tables made from orange crates and packing boxes, old rugs on the stone floor, some sleeping bags, electric lanterns, boxes of crackers and candy, a bus-stop sign, a broken motorcycle, two old car doors, parts of uniforms, and a lot more junk.

"It looks like—" Pete started.

"—a clubhouse!" Bob finished. "It's his gang's hideout!"

"Of course," Jupiter whispered. "Just where he'd hide anything he didn't want found. Careful, fellows, he's here somewhere."

They stood up quietly in the dim cave and moved ahead, crouched low. Some ten yards farther on the cave curved sharply left. Around the curve, Frankie Bender was kneeling in front of a flat rock. On the rock, open, was a small black carrying case!

Bender heard the boys, and turned in alarm.

"So you have it!" Jupiter said.

The alarm left the bully boy's face, and was replaced by a dazed expression.

"It's . . . it's . . . gone!"

The boys ran forward. The black case was lined with heavy blue velvet—and was empty!

"It was a statue," Frankie Bender babbled. "This swell statue! A real great mascot for our gang. Some kind of crazy figure—"

"What did it look like—exactly!" Jupiter demanded.

Bender was facing them. His eyes suddenly grew wide with terror.

"It looked"—he pointed behind the boys—"like *that!*"

The Investigators whirled around.

"Ulp!" Pete choked.

The apparition from the beach stood in the dim cave!

"The statue," Frankie Bender moaned, "it's come alive!"

Jangling and stamping, the shaggy thing with the great horned head and red eyes began to dance toward them!

9

Trapped!

Paralyzed, the four boys stood in the dim cave with nowhere to run. The monstrous thing capered toward them, its slit-eyes glowing red.

The cave ended behind them. They were trapped!

"Jupe, what do we do?" Bob cried.

"I . . . I don't—" Jupiter stammered.

It was Frank Bender who suddenly acted. He was a bully, but he had courage. White-faced, he pulled out his slingshot, picked up a heavy stone from the cave floor, and shot it at the advancing apparition. Hit, the savage figure grunted and fell back a step. Bender grabbed more stones.

"Throw rocks, you guys!" he yelled.

Pete and Bob grabbed larger stones and hurled them at the savage demon figure. Bender kept on shooting his slingshot. But the hail of missiles bounced off the thick padding and huge head of the creature with no apparent damage.

It shook its shaggy head. *"Ahhhhrrrrrrr!"* it groaned, and began to move faster as the boys retreated to the back wall.

"We can't hurt it!" Frankie Bender cried.

The barbarous figure danced closer in the dim cave.

Jupiter moved. He darted to the black case, still lying open on the flat rock, and grabbed it. Holding it in one hand, he picked up a large stone and held it over the open case.

"I'll smash it!" he cried.

The eerie apparition stopped dead! Its red slit-eyes burned toward Jupiter, but it stood motionless. Jupiter stared at it, his eyes glinting.

"So you're real enough to understand English," he said.

"And he sure wants the statue!" Bob added.

"Why not?" Frankie Bender said, his voice shaking. "He *is* the statue. Or the statue's *him*. Or . . . maybe . . ."

The apparition began to quiver slowly where it stood. The bells, bones, rattles that hung from its neck and belt jangled and rattled as if some great force surged inside. The flat, hollow voice filled the cave:

"Small creatures, beware. Defilers are destroyed."

Jupiter held the rock over the black case. "What is this statue? Who are you?"

"Hear the Spirit Shaman, fools!" the hollow voice boomed. *"The Great Khan of the Golden Horde waits in the wind for the Dancing Devil!"*

Pete gulped. "Dancing Devil? Khan? Golden—what?"

"The statue is the Dancing Devil?" Jupiter said, watching the monster. "Or you are? A spirit that speaks English?"

"We are one, and we are all! We see all, know all! We are

the blue sky, the golden sun, the endless steppe, the sword, and the corn! We destroy in the flame of the wind. Behold!"

Its heavy arm swept forward, pointing to the flat rock. There was a flash of flame, a thick puff of white smoke!

"Watch out!" Frankie Bender yelled, jumping away.

"Tremble!" the hollow voice intoned.

The creature's arm flicked again, and a flash of flame and smoke burst from the cave floor not five feet from Pete!

"The Great Khan waits for what is his!"

Shaking, the four boys jumped back until they were pinned against the rear wall of the cave. The apparition leveled its long arm straight at them and began to advance again. Jupiter threw away the stone he was holding over the open case.

"Here!" the First Investigator cried. "Take it!"

He snapped the case shut and heaved it as far as he could across the dim cave. The thing, spirit, Dancing Devil, or whatever it was, gave a loud cry and jumped toward the black case as it crashed to the ground among stacks of clubhouse junk.

"Now, guys!" Jupiter yelled.

The others didn't need any urging. As the Dancing Devil went after the case, the boys fled past him for the cave mouth. If the Devil saw their flight, it didn't seem to care. It was intent only on searching the shadows for the case.

The fleeing boys stumbled over orange crates and packing boxes, and fell over each other as they scrambled out the entrance to the cave.

Outside, they burst through the thick mesquite that ripped at their clothes. With Frankie Bender in the lead and Jupiter puffing in the rear, they tumbled slipping and sliding down the steep slope all the way to the bottom of the mountain.

They landed in a heap in a shallow barranca and lay there panting against the bank, hidden from above. For some minutes none of them moved or spoke. Breathing hard, they listened for the sound of pursuit.

There was only silence on the hot mountain.

"Don't forget on the beach!" Pete panted. "He can show up almost anywhere!"

Huddled in the gully, the boys listened. They heard nothing. Finally they cautiously raised their heads over the edge of the barranca to search the dry slope and brush. None of them saw anything, and on up the mountain nothing came through the mesquite at the cave mouth.

"Where is he . . . it . . . whatever?" Frankie Bender asked.

"I'm not so sure I want to know," Pete said. "Jupe?"

The First Investigator didn't answer, but went on watching the mesquite that hid the mouth of the cave. Half an hour later, still no one and nothing had come out. Jupiter stood up.

"We have to go back up there," he announced.

"You're crazy!" Frank Bender cried. "I'm leaving."

"I think you'll come with us, Bender," Jupiter said firmly. "Or you can talk to the police about how you got the statue."

Bender became sullen but said nothing. He followed as the Investigators climbed cautiously back up the slope to the cave. Inside, the cave was silent. Stepping warily, the boys went all around the dim interior. It was empty, and the black case was gone. Where they had last seen the Dancing Devil, they found two small piles of the white ash. Pete touched them. The ashes were barely warm now.

"Is there another way out?" Jupiter asked.

"No," Frankie Bender said. "So how did that Devil thing get out?"

"It turned to smoke and blew away," Pete said.

"Or it slipped out while we were running," Jupiter said. "We didn't look back up here for some time."

"Anyway," Bob said dejectedly, "it won't be after us any more. The thief's got the statue, so the Devil won't hang around. I guess the case is over for us."

"On the contrary, Records," Jupiter snapped. "I'm quite sure that the thief doesn't have the statue! In fact, he has less idea than ever where it is now."

"Gosh," Pete said. "How do you figure that, First?"

"The Dancing Devil is obviously connected to the small thief," Jupiter explained. "So if the thief had taken the statue from the cave, the Devil wouldn't have been tailing us, and he would have known the case had to be empty! He didn't know, so someone else must have the statue." The First Investigator turned to Frank Bender. "Has anyone been around the cave recently besides your gang, Frankie?"

The barrel-chested boy hesitated. Now that the danger was over, his bullying antagonism had come back.

"You stole that statue, Bender. We can make a lot of trouble for you," Jupiter said coldly. "Cooperate, and we'll keep quiet."

Frankie scowled, but nodded. "There was a guy, an old hobo. He used to use this cave before we chased him off. I saw him around here yesterday, and I found a wine bottle in here today."

"What's his name?" Bob demanded.

"Don't know, but he's easy to spot. Maybe seventy, has a white beard, weighs two hundred pounds, always wears cowboy boots and an old Navy coat."

"No more tricks, Frankie," Jupiter warned. "Fellows!"

They left Bender in the cave, and hurried down the mountain and through the sunny town back to Pete's house. It was time for lunch, but Jupiter wasn't thinking of food.

"A hobo!" he exclaimed. "Pete, remember that drifter who sells junk to the yard? The guitar player, Andy? The one Uncle Titus says is a genius, but who likes to just wander? He knows every hobo around. After lunch, you and Bob go to Headquarters and call all the places he hangs out in and find him!"

"Right, First," Pete said. "What are you going to do?"

Jupiter's eyes gleamed. "I'm going to track down a Great Khan, a Golden Horde, and the Dancing Devil!"

10

The Dancing Devil of Batu Khan

"Fellows," Jupiter said, "meet the Dancing Devil!"

It was early afternoon. The Investigators were gathered once more in their hidden trailer headquarters. Bob and Pete had been making calls to locate the drifter, Andy, and had left word everywhere that Jupiter wanted him to come to the salvage yard.

They were still calling when Jupiter climbed up through the trap door carrying a large book. Excited, he laid the book open on the desk, pointed to a picture, and made his startling announcement. Bob and Pete peered at the photograph in the book.

"It's the statue!" Bob realized.

"It's that . . . thing we keep seeing, too," Pete groaned.

The picture showed a small statue of a wildly dancing figure, about fourteen inches from its head to the base of the pedestal. Made of green metal, the figure stood on one bent leg, with the other leg in the air and its arms flung wide. With its shaggy head, spreading horns, hanging wolf skin, and padded arms and legs, the statue was a miniature of the eerie apparition!

There was a text under the picture. Bob began to read: " 'The Dancing Devil of Batu Khan. Found in northern China in the late nineteenth century, when it was given its popular name. The bronze statue is dated 1241 A.D. and inscribed in Latin "To the Exalted Khan of the Golden Horde." Obviously the work of a European artisan, it may have been a tribute to, or a magical charm against, Batu Khan. The depiction of a Mongol shaman, it wears a wolf skin and a mask with yak horns, and is festooned with bells, rattles, bones, and bunches of grass, corn and roots to symbolise the spirits of the natural universe.' " Bob looked up. "Gee, Jupe, what does that all mean?"

"It means it's so valuable it's just about priceless!"

Pete peered at the photo. "Gee, I didn't know bronze was worth so much."

"It's not a matter of *what* the statue is made of, Second. It's *when* it was made, and *why*," Jupiter said. "When that demon thing talked about the Golden Horde and shamans, I decided to go see Professor Hsiang from the university. He's an expert on Oriental art, and he recognized the Devil as soon as I described it! He—"

"What *is* the Golden Horde?" Pete wanted to know. "Sounds like a Big Ten football team. And who was Batu Khan?"

"You've heard of Genghis Khan? Or maybe Kublai

Khan?"

"Well," Pete said, doubtfully. "They were kings or something. Big generals, like Napoleon and Alexander the Great, right? Wasn't Kublai Khan the guy that Marco Polo went to see in China? I guess they must have been Chinese emperors."

"The khans were Oriental, but not Chinese—even though Kublai was emperor of China. They were Mongols—nomads from the north of China. The Mongols were horsemen, warrior horsemen. They lived in tents and moved around in small tribes. In fact, some of them still live that way up there. But now, part of the Mongolian territory belongs to China."

"So they're not Chinese, and they like horses and fighting. What's that got to do with the statue?"

"About the year 1206, Genghis Khan put a bunch of the tribes together, mostly by beating them and taking over, and started to conquer the whole world! Before he and his sons and grandsons were finished, they owned everything north of India from Korea in the east to Hungary in the west! They ruled Siberia, China, Russia, Persia, and much of eastern Europe. The sons had names like Juchi, Ogadai, and Chagatai. Kublai Khan was a grandson and so was Batu."

"Wow," Pete said, "even their names sound tough."

"They *were* tough," Jupiter said. "They slaughtered everybody who tried to resist them. Batu Khan was the one who beat the Russians and Hungarians, and ruled the westernmost part of the Mongol Empire. His army—and his part of the empire—was called the Golden Horde. The Mongols were better warriors than they were rulers, so the empire didn't last long. But the Golden Horde existed in Russia until 1480."

"Okay, but what about the statue?" asked Pete. "And that shaman business?"

"Well," Jupe continued, "Batu Khan's religion—the Mongol religion—is called shamanism. The Mongols believe that there are spirits in the rocks, wind, sky, earth, and trees, and that a special man can talk to the spirits—the shaman."

"Hey," Bob said, "like an Indian medicine man."

"Exactly! In fact, the American Indians were originally Asiatic people and probably have the same ancestors as the Mongols. Anyway, Professor Hsiang told me a lot about the shamans. They were experts in ventriloquism, and they called on the spirits by dancing! Some of the shamans—the most powerful ones—could even call on demons! The shamans always wore a disguise during their rituals, so the spirits wouldn't know who they really were. They covered themselves with masks and animal skins, just as the statue shows."

"So what's so special about the statue?" asked Pete.

"There's nothing else like it in the world!" answered Jupiter. "You see, the Mongols didn't make statues—at least not permanent ones. They had idols—images of their deities —but those were made out of clay and felt and other things that don't last. This metal statue was created by a European artist. It's the only permanent example of a Mongolian figure. It's unique!"

"I wonder how it ever got to China?" mused Bob. "You said the statue belonged to Batu, and he ruled in the West."

"Nobody knows, Records. Professor Hsiang told me that Batu didn't stay around Russia all the time. The capital of the empire was back in Mongolia at Karakorum. That's where Russian princes had to go to swear loyalty to the Grand Khan—the emperor. Batu had to quit fighting in 1242 and go back there himself to help elect a Grand Khan after the old one died. Maybe he took the statue with him, and left it there for some reason. About forty years later, Kublai Khan took over China and became the Grand Khan and moved the Mongol capital to what's now Peking. Maybe the statue was sent on to there. We'll never know exactly what happened."

"Well, do you know how the statue got over here?"

"Read the rest of the caption, Records."

Bob read aloud, " 'The statue remained in China until World War II, then vanished during the Japanese occupation. In 1956 it reappeared in London, where it was bought by the wealthy American H. P. Clay, and placed in his private collection of Oriental art.' "

"H. P. Clay?" Pete said. "Isn't that the oil tycoon who has the mansion down on Fernand Point? You mean, the statue's been in Rocky Beach for twenty years? Then the thief—"

"Must have stolen it right here!" Jupiter finished. "I think we'd better go and talk to Mr. H. P. Clay!"

In case Andy should show up, the boys left word with Konrad, one of the big Bavarian brothers who worked in the salvage yard, that they were going to the Clay mansion. They biked off and turned south on the coast road.

"Jupe?" Pete said suddenly as they rode through the heavy beach traffic. "We know what the statue is, but what is that live Dancing Devil?"

"Well, the Mongols still believe in shamanism, at least a

lot of them do, so maybe it's a real shaman looking for the statue. Professor Hsiang says the Chinese now want it back. They asked our President to help get it returned when he last visited Peking. So maybe a shaman is putting on some pressure. Or else—"

"Or else what, Jupe?"

"The Mongols believe there's a spirit in everything," Jupiter said. "Perhaps we saw the spirit of the Dancing Devil."

"I shouldn't have asked," Pete moaned.

Jupiter and Bob laughed, but even they wondered uneasily just what they'd seen. None of the boys said anything more until they reached Fernand Point, where the coast curved out to sea. It was a wild, hilly, wooded area of some twenty acres with no buildings in sight behind a high iron fence.

The iron gates were open, and the three boys biked up the long curving driveway until they came into sight of a mansion across a vast lawn. It was a massive two-story Moorish-style building with white walls, dark brown beams, a red tile roof, and long rows of small windows behind ornate iron grillwork.

Jupiter stepped up to imposing double doors and rang. He seemed to grow taller as he assumed his most dignified manner. An elderly man in a formal coat and striped trousers answered—the butler. He looked the boys up and down severely.

"Yes, young man?"

"Mr. Jupiter Jones, my good man," Jupiter said in his best aristocratic drawl. "Calling on Mr. H. P. Clay."

"I see," the butler said with a faint smile. "I regret, Mr.

Jones, but Mr. Clay is not at home."

"It's quite urgent," Jupiter insisted. "May I ask where Mr. Clay could be reached at once?"

A voice spoke from inside, "Who is it, Stevens?"

"A Jupiter Jones for your father, Master James."

A tall, smiling young man of no more than twenty appeared beside the butler. He grinned at the boys.

"My dad's out of town. Maybe I could handle it?"

Jupiter hesitated. "Well—"

"Come on into the library," James Clay said. "You can leave them with me now, Stevens."

The butler nodded and walked away. The tall young man led the boys into a large book-lined room.

"Okay, fellows, we can talk here," he said. "What's it all about?"

"It's about the Dancing Devil, Mr. Clay," Jupiter said.

"Call me Jim," he said. "What about the Devil?"

Pete blurted out, "It's been stolen!"

"Stolen?" Jim Clay shook his head. "Oh, no. I saw it only three or four days ago. I remember, because—"

"It was stolen two days ago," Bob said quickly.

"Two days?" He eyed him. "All right, let's go and see."

He took them down broad hallways to the rear of the house and unlocked a heavy set of double doors with a key on his chain. They stepped into a large, dimly lit room cluttered with shapes, and . . .

Half-crouched, a figure with a shaggy horned head and red slit-eyes stared straight toward them across the dim room, its gaping mouth open and a wolf skin hanging down!

11

An Unexpected Face

"It's—it's . . . here!" Jupiter stuttered.

Rigidly, the boys faced the apparition.

The lights went on!

"What is it? What's here?" Jim Clay said, his voice puzzled as he looked around the cluttered room.

"The Dancing Devil!" Pete pointed. "There, you see—"

His voice trailed off as he stared at the motionless figure standing crouched on a low pedestal. Jim Clay walked to it and tapped it. It was hard and hollow.

"Oh, no," he said, "the Dancing Devil is bronze and much smaller. This is just a mannequin with a Mongol shaman costume on it. My dad collects Oriental arts and crafts. This outfit is completely authentic, fellows."

Jupiter walked slowly across the room, skirting glass display cases, and touched the costume on the mannequin. A cloud of dust rose. The First Investigator stepped back, nodding.

"I can see now that it's different," he said. "The horns are a lot shorter, and the skin is a bear's, not a wolf's. Besides, the dust shows it hasn't been moved in a long time."

"Different from what, Jupiter?" Jim Clay asked.

"The shaman costume, or real shaman, or whatever it is we've been seeing," Pete said. "Does your dad maybe have another shaman outfit around?"

"Only that one. They're pretty rare, I guess," Jim Clay said.

"Ours is exactly like the Dancing Devil," Bob said.

"Well, maybe the statue came to life." The tycoon's son grinned. "The real statue's over there in that glass case."

He stared. The glass case was empty!

"It *is* gone!" Pete cried.

Jim Clay looked around, confused. He hurried through the big room, looking in every glass case. There were other statues, weapons, vases, helmets, and many other works of arts and crafts, but the Dancing Devil wasn't there!

"I . . . I don't understand! How could anyone—?" He turned to the boys. "How did you three know it was gone?"

They told him everything that had happened. The young man listened closely, watching them, and then began to pace. His voice was distraught.

"Stolen! When I was supposed to be keeping an eye on things! My dad will be furious! The statue's priceless, and besides . . ." He stopped, and shook his head. "I'm not much interested in the Oriental stuff, so I didn't particularly look out for the statue, you know? But how could a thief get in here and take it without being seen or leaving a trail? I've been busy with my college work, but Stevens should have seen anyone, or Quail—" He turned quickly to the telephone and pressed a button. "Quail? Come to the Collection Room."

Clay hung up and went on pacing. "You say the thief *lost* the statue? Then it could be anywhere! My dad's going to have a fit. He left me in charge a week ago, and he'll—"

The door opened, and a man came in. Jim Clay turned.

"Ah, Quail! Something terrible—"

Pete's eyes widened. "It's him!"

Bob and Jupiter froze. It was the thin man in the rimless glasses! Jim Clay looked at the newcomer and the boys.

"What?" he said, mystified. "Quail is who?"

"Who is this man, Jim?" Jupiter said slowly.

"My dad's literary assistant, Walter Quail. He helps my dad to write articles about his collection. Why?"

"Because he's the man we told you about who stopped us from chasing the thief, and who was in the thief's motel room!" Bob said.

Jim Clay turned on the assistant. "Quail?"

"Yes," Walter Quail said, "it's true. I observed this strange rat-faced little man hanging about the house and grounds. I was suspicious, so I followed him. When those boys told me he was a thief, I continued to follow him. However, I lost him at that motel. I searched the motel room, but found nothing."

"So you knew that the Dancing Devil had been stolen?"

"Stolen!" He seemed startled. The twitch in his left eye became more pronounced. Then he looked toward the empty glass case and slowly nodded. "Yes, I knew. I—"

Jupiter watched Quail, his face alert and puzzled. But Jim Clay broke in impatiently.

"Why didn't you tell me?" he snapped. "Did you tell the police? Or my father?"

"No, James, I haven't told the police yet, or anyone," Quail said, and looked toward the boys. "It could be a very touchy matter, as you know."

Young Clay chewed his lip. "Yes, the Chinese."

"It could be a large scandal for your father," Quail said.

"But we have to do something!" Jim Clay insisted. "Maybe a private detective agency!"

"I'm not sure they are very trustworthy," Quail said, "and I know your father wouldn't want too many people to know."

"Jim?" Jupiter said quickly, "We know some private detectives who know all about the Dancing Devil theft already."

"What?" the youth said. "Who, Jupiter?"

"Us!" Bob and Pete cried in unison.

Jupiter dug a business card out of his pocket and handed it to Clay. The young man and Walter Quail studied it.

THE THREE INVESTIGATORS
"We Investigate Anything"
?   ?   ?

First Investigator . . . . Jupiter Jones
Second Investigator . . . . Peter Crenshaw
Records and Research . . . . Bob Andrews

"We were hired to work on the case by one of the thief's

other victims," Jupiter said. "But we've solved that part."

"Child detectives?" Quail sneered.

"Show him our other card, First!" Pete said hotly.

Jim Clay read the second card. It said:

> *This certifies that the bearer is a*
> *Volunteer Junior Assistant Deputy*
> *cooperating with the police force of*
> *Rocky Beach. Any assistance given*
> *him will be appreciated.*
>   (Signed) *Samuel Reynolds*
>   *Chief of Police*

The tycoon's son looked up. "It certainly sounds as if you fellows are authentic, and you do know all about this. Time is very important, and if I work with—"

"Ridiculous, James!" Quail snapped. "Your father—"

Jupiter said, "We already know where to look next, Jim. We have a solid lead," and he told the youth about the old hobo.

"That settles it," Jim Clay decided. "I'll go with you, and right now!" He turned to Walter Quail. "Unless you think we should call the police in, Walter?"

Quail hesitated. "No, James, perhaps you're right."

The prim assistant turned and walked out of the room. Jim Clay grinned, and Jupiter stared after Quail.

"How long has he worked for your father, Jim?" Jupiter asked.

"About two years," Clay said. "You're not thinking—?"

"There is often an inside connection," Jupiter said grimly.

"Did you notice how he started to act surprised when you told him the Devil had been stolen? Then changed his mind?"

"I noticed," Jim Clay admitted. "It's funny he just followed the thief without trying to stop him, and why didn't he call the police?" The tycoon's son frowned. "Of course, it *is* a very sensitive matter. My dad would want it kept quiet."

"Why?" Jupiter said. "Because the Chinese Government wants the statue returned, and the theft could cause an international incident?"

"I see you are a good detective," Clay said. "Yes, the Chinese Communists have wanted the statue back for a long time, but until recently our government didn't care. But now our government wants to be friends with Red China, so they've asked my dad to return the statue. He wanted to keep it—he bought it honestly—but the President personally asked him to give it up. My dad finally agreed. He's in Washington right now arranging for a Chinese Communist official to come and get it. He's due back any day, and if the Devil isn't here there could be trouble with China. Everyone knows Dad hates to lose it."

"Then we'd better get it back," Jupiter said stoutly.

"Yes," Jim Clay said. His eyes narrowed. "Fellows, what did you say the thief looks like?"

"What?" Jupiter said. "Well, he's small and thin, with a skinny face—"

"Like that?" the young man said, pointing to the window.

A face stared in at the window—a long, lean face with bright, burning eyes, long red hair down to the shoulders, and a sharp, satanic red beard!

12

The Thief Reappears

The devilish red beard split in a grin outside the window.

"It's Andy!" Pete cried. "Go around to the door, Andy!" he cried.

Andy disappeared and was shortly ushered into the Collection Room by the butler.

"Hi, guys," he said with a big smile. Then, before Jupe could introduce him to Jim Clay, Andy saw all the Oriental art treasures in the room. "Hey, far out!"

He began to walk around the room. "A real Mongol shaman costume! Look, a Ming vase, and it's real! A Sung tapestry, a Ch'ing jade lion, a T'ang Buddha! All real!"

Andy was about twenty-five, tall and handsome. He wore an old fringed Indian-style shirt over torn and patched corduroy pants and high moccasins. A guitar was slung over his back, and a huge silver medallion hung on a chain at the open throat of his shirt. It swung as he walked around eagerly studying the collection.

"Beautiful!" he enthused. "The greatest!"

Jim Clay blinked at Andy's clothes and guitar. "You know Oriental art, Mr.—?"

"Call me Andy," the young wanderer said.

"Andy has a master's degree in fine arts," Jupiter explained.

"I like to live free," Andy said, looking at the tycoon's son. "No house, no car, no furniture, no nine-to-five job. Go where I want and when I want, to do what I want." He eyed Jim Clay. "You're H. P. Clay's kid? Your father and I don't think much alike. How do you think?"

"My father's a very successful man!" Jim Clay said.

"Depends what you call success," Andy said. "Look at all this beautiful stuff here. It's great to make it, and look at it, but it's a crime to collect it in a room and hide it."

"My dad bought it all fair and square!" Jim Clay snapped.

"He should give it away—give it back to the people it belongs to," Andy snapped back. Then he grinned. "But you all didn't want to see me to hear a lecture. What's up, Jupe?"

Jupiter told the young wanderer about the old hobo Frankie Bender had seen at the cave.

"I know him. We call him the Chief," Andy said. "He always wears the jacket of a chief petty officer in the Navy."

"Do you know where he is now?" Jim Clay asked.

"Maybe," Andy said, looking at the boys. "What do you want him for?"

"We've been hired—" Bob started to say.

Jim Clay interrupted him. "Excuse me, but I'd like to talk

to you boys privately for a moment."

Andy shot an amused look at the tycoon's son, shrugged, and moved off to browse through the art treasures.

"Listen," said Jim quickly to the Investigators. "I wouldn't tell him about the Dancing Devil. The fewer people who know about the theft, the better."

Jupiter frowned. "I don't think Andy will help us find that hobo unless we give a good reason for wanting him," he said. "And it might take us days to find the hobo on our own."

Jim looked doubtful. "Well, your friend doesn't seem to have any respect for my dad. Are you sure he can be trusted?"

"Definitely," answered Jupe. "And I'm sure he'll be happy to help us once we tell him the whole story. You heard what he just said about returning art to the people it belongs to!"

Jim laughed ruefully. "Okay, go ahead and fill him in."

Jupiter was right. Andy was eager to help retrieve the stolen statue so it could go back to China.

"I guess I spoke too soon about your father," he admitted to Jim Clay. "Your old man is sure doing one good thing now. You say my hobo friend might have seen that statue last? Okay, let's go find him!"

"Is he far away?" Jim Clay asked.

"Could be far or near," Andy said. "The Chief moves around just like I do."

"Then we can take my station wagon," Jim said as they went out. "The boys can load their bikes in the back."

It was a big Buick Estate Wagon. Andy directed young Clay to the railroad yards. There were hobos around the yard, but The Chief wasn't among them. They didn't know where he was. Andy shook his head as they drove on toward the Bird Refuge.

"We better leave this overpowered chariot out of sight," he said. "It makes the guys suspicious, and they won't talk."

Even with the Buick out of sight up the road, none of the hobos at the Bird Refuge knew anything about The Chief.

Next, they went up the coast to a state beach where transients and drifters gathered in a secluded wooded area beyond the picnic grounds. Andy went alone this time and came back quickly.

"The Chief may be at the camp near the county dump!"

Jim drove inland across the freeway and into the brown foothills where the county dump lay. It was a noisy, smelly area. Giant bulldozers rumbled over piles of refuse, and hundreds of seagulls screamed as they swirled and swooped over the garbage. The hobo camp was across the road from the dump, down in a broad valley full of brush.

They left the Buick at the top of the valley, and walked down a dirt road to where hobos sat in front of a cluster of rickety shacks. Andy went and spoke to the men. One of them pointed toward the last shack. Andy beckoned to Jim and the boys and hurried toward the hut at the end. He bent and went in through the low doorway. The others followed.

"Chief?" Andy was saying. "Wake up, old buddy!"

As their eyes became accustomed to the gloom inside, the boys saw the old man lying on a torn mattress. He had a ragged white beard, wore the jacket of a chief petty officer and cowboy boots, and smiled up at Andy as he opened his eyes. He waved his hand. There was money in it.

"Little rest, Andy me boy!" he said, closing his eyes again.

"Chief?" Andy said. "Where'd you get the money?"

"Share it with you, me boy," the old man said, his eyes still closed. "Found something. Lucky. Shhhhhhhhhhhh—!"

Jim Clay stepped forward, kicking an empty wine bottle out of the way. "You found a statue in that cave! What did you do with the statue?"

The Chief's eyes opened in alarm. He looked scared. Andy patted his shoulder. The old man smiled and closed his eyes again.

"It's okay, Chief. No one's going to bother you. We just want to know what you did with the statue. You sold it, right?"

"Perhaps," Jupiter said, "a small reward would help?"

The Chief's eyes opened. "Reward?"

"Ten dollars," Jim Clay said quickly, taking out a ten-dollar bill. "And no trouble. Who did you sell the statue to?"

"Found it. My cave, you know? Last night," the old man said, nodding to himself. "Sold it this morning. The junk shop. You know, Andy boy? The place we sells to." He chuckled. "Fooled old Fritz this time. Gave me twenty bucks!"

"Twenty dollars?" Jim Clay groaned. "Where is the shop?"

"Hummer's Curio Shop at the harbor," Andy said. "We sell a lot of old things we find to Fritz Hummer."

"Reward!" The Chief said, his hand out.

Jim Clay handed him the ten, then turned to the low door. "Ask what else he knows! Has anyone else been around? I'll go and get the car so we don't waste any more time!"

As the young man ran out, Andy turned back to The Chief, who was grinning at the new ten-dollar bill in his gnarled hand.

"Chief? Can you tell us anything else about the statue?"

"Has anyone else been asking about it?" Jupiter asked.

The old man shook his head back and forth, then began to blink and search the mattress as if he'd lost something. He saw the ten-dollar bill in his hand, and smiled at it.

"Think, Chief!" Andy urged. "Anyone looking for you?"

The old man shook his head, slowly lay back with his eyes shut again, and began to snore. Andy motioned the boys outside. The other hobos glanced curiously at them, then looked away. The station wagon wasn't in sight yet. Jupiter looked back at the shack thoughtfully.

"I wonder if the Curio Shop owner had any idea of the statue's real value?" he said.

"I doubt it, Jupe," Andy said. "He sells mostly junk."

Then the Buick came bouncing along the dirt road. Andy and the boys piled in, and Jim Clay drove off spurting gravel. He reached the freeway and sped toward the harbor. But once they were off the freeway, he had to slow down drastically. Traffic was heavy in downtown Rocky Beach. The Buick crawled toward the waterfront.

The Curio Shop turned out to be some distance from the public parking lot. "You fellows better go ahead while I park!" Jim decided. He dropped them at a nearby corner and drove off.

The Curio Shop was in a row of stores with alleys between them leading back to the marina. Walking quickly down the block, Andy and the boys caught glimpses of boats and

sparkling water as they passed the alleys. A man was standing at the far end of the alley next to the Curio Shop. Pete
glanced at him briefly, then did a double take.

"In the alley! It's the thief!"

The Investigators saw the rat-faced man peering at them.
The small man still wore his cape. It billowed out as he
turned and ran.

"After him, fellows!" Bob yelled.

Through the narrow alley between the shops, they raced
out to the edge of the harbor and the marina full of boats.

"There he is!" Andy spotted him.

The thief was running along a wooden dock that projected
perpendicularly from the harbor's edge. He clambered
aboard a cabin cruiser tied alongside the dock and vanished
into the enclosed wheelhouse. Andy and the boys ran for the
boat. Pete pointed to an open hatch near the bow.

"I'll cut him off up forward," he cried.

Jupiter, Bob, and Andy leaped onto the boat and ran into
the wheelhouse. The thief was nowhere in sight. The door
to the cabin below was open.

"Careful, guys," Andy warned as they went slowly down
the ladderlike stairs.

In the cabin below they saw no sign of the thief. They
moved on into the forward cabin. Pete met them there.

"He didn't pass me!" the Second Investigator declared.

"He's tricked us!" Jupiter realized. "He's still up in—"

There was a loud bang as the door to the wheelhouse
closed and locked with a click. They whirled toward the
forward hatch. It slammed down, and the sound of its being
locked echoed through the silence below deck.

13

The Greedy Fat Man

Up on deck footsteps ran away, and the boat rocked gently as someone leaped off it onto the dock. Silence settled on the yacht. In the locked cabin, the Investigators stood in dismay.

"Well," Andy said, shrugging, "he sure suckered us good."

"He must have been hiding in the wheelhouse," Bob said woefully. "In a locker or something. He sure outsmarted us."

"Or trapped us," Jupiter said. "I doubt that he could have hidden so well, small as he is, without knowing ahead of time exactly where to hide. I think he had this operation planned!"

"Well, he sure left us in a comfortable place," Andy pointed out. He looked appreciatively around the luxurious cabin. It was a combination living-sleeping cabin at the stern end of the boat. Cushioned benches were built in under the portholes on each side. They obviously served for seating during the day and sleeping at night. A table was anchored to the floor in the middle of the cabin with easy chairs around it. Oiled teakwood trim gleamed softly everywhere.

"Hey, look at that!" said Andy, pointing to the little passageway between the stern cabin and the forward sleeping quarters. On each side of it was a narrow door with a neat printed sign. One said "Galley" and one said "Head." "A kitchen and a bath. I'll betcha there's food stockpiled. All our needs have been provided for!" Smiling, the bearded young man unslung his guitar, stretched out on a bench, and began to play "Yo, ho, ho and a bottle of rum!"

"Andy, how can you lie there playing like that!" demanded Pete hotly. "We're trapped in here and we've got to get out!"

"How? We're too big to wriggle through the portholes. Don't worry, the owner or somebody will show up eventually. You know, Pete," said Andy kindly, "you strike me as the kind of guy who dies three times."

"What!" exclaimed Pete, shocked.

"I mean, you worry about things ahead of time, then you suffer while they happen, then you can't stop brooding about them afterwards. Now me, I just take things as they come. So we're stuck down here? Relax and enjoy it!"

"Never mind that!" snapped Jupiter, suddenly exasperated with his easygoing friend. "While we stand here talking, that thief is going after the statue. Maybe he's got it already! We've got to find a way out of here—and quickly!"

"You're the boss!" said Andy obligingly. "What shall we do?"

"Bob, you take the portholes. See if anyone is within yelling distance. Pete, try up forward for an open hatchway. Andy, check this cabin. Sometimes there's a service hatch. I'll see if the wheelhouse door is breakable!"

Pete was the first to complete his assignment. He returned, shaking his head—there were no hatches forward that would open from below. Andy found no way out in the stern, and Jupiter had to report that the wheelhouse door was stoutly locked with no way to get room enough to throw weight against it.

"First!" Bob was looking out a small porthole on the side opposite to the dock. "I thought I saw that assistant! Walter Quail!"

They all hurried to portholes. Across the rows of boats in the marina, far down on the harborside esplanade, a figure was half-hidden. Pete and Jupiter squinted to see clearly in the low sunlight that reflected off the water.

"I . . . I'm not sure," Pete said. "It could be."

"He's wearing glasses and looking this way!" Bob said.

"Yes," Jupiter agreed, "and he seems to be trying not to be seen. Do you see the Mercedes he drives?"

They strained to make out the Mercedes among all the cars parked in the distance.

"I can see Jim's Estate Wagon," Bob said.

"Where *is* Jim?" Pete wondered.

"That man's leaving!" Jupiter cried. "Is it Quail?" None of them could be sure.

Suddenly Andy spotted another figure emerging onto the esplanade.

"Hey, isn't that Jim Clay over there? Coming out of the alley?"

The Investigators switched their gazes, and let out sighs of relief.

"Hey, Jim!" "Here we are, Jim!" The boys pulled open portholes and began yelling and waving.

Jim seemed too far away to hear them. He stood looking around the marina, then moved uncertainly in their direction. His mouth was open as if he were calling. Finally the Investigators heard his voice across the water.

"Jupiter! Bob! Where are you? Pete!"

"In here!" Pete yelled. "The big boat!" He waved frantically and finally caught Jim's eye.

Jim started to run in their direction. He passed out of their line of sight—and then pounding footsteps sounded on the wooden dock. Jim's face appeared at a dockside porthole.

"We're locked in!" Bob cried.

"Hold on!"

There was a banging and rattling in the wheelhouse, and then the cabin door was flung open. The boys and Andy climbed up into the open where Jim Clay stood anxiously. "What happened, fellows?" he asked.

They told him, and Pete said, "That thief has probably got the Devil back, and run off!"

"Maybe not," Jim said grimly. "I was out in front of that Curio Shop for a while, and I didn't see anyone like him."

"Then perhaps there's still time!" Jupiter said.

Jim whirled and ran back through the alley with the others behind him. They hurried into the Curio Shop. In the late afternoon of a weekday, only a few tourists were still browsing in the seedy shop. Gimcracks and junk, gleaned from fire sales, secondhand dealers, and Hong Kong manufacturers, were piled everywhere.

A short fat man in a dirty sweater sat behind a counter, smoking a smelly pipe. His eyes glittered greedily at the tourists. He turned with an oily smile as the boys, Jim, and Andy came in. When he saw Andy, his smile faded.

"Hobo time is after hours," the fat man snarled, and glared at the boys. "And no kids in here, no time! Out!"

"You, my man, serve the public," Jupiter said sharply, looking his most imperious. "Discrimination by age is illegal, as I suspect are other practices of yours. Our card!"

The fat man sat stunned by Jupiter's flow of words, and took the card the First Investigator held out. Andy smiled.

"Better read it, Fritz, and watch yourself," he said.

It was the card from Chief Reynolds appointing the boys Junior Assistant Deputies. The fat man paled as he read it, but tried to bluster.

"I got nothin' to hide, and no kids—"

Jim Clay stepped close to the fat man. "I expect you've got a lot to hide, but never mind that. My name is James L. Clay the Third. Are you going to tell me to leave?"

"C–C–Clay?" Fritz Hummer stuttered. "You mean H. P. Clay's—?"

"Son, yes," Jim snapped. "Now can we stay and talk?"

Fritz Hummer nodded eagerly, wiped his greasy hands on his sweater. "Of course, Mr. Clay. What can I do for all of you, ah, gentlemen?"

The tourists had left hurriedly during the argument, and now the shop was empty except for Hummer and the boys, Jim, and Andy.

"You can sell us the statue you bought from The Chief,"

Pete blurted out.

"Statue?" Hummer seemed puzzled. Then his eyes lighted. "Ah, yes, that dancing figure with the horns. Nice piece."

"Just a sentimental item," Jupiter said quickly. "You do have it, don't you? We're willing to pay a reasonable price."

"Well," Hummer said, "I'm not sure. I sold—"

Jim Clay scowled angrily. "It's mine, Hummer, and I want it back! You hear? Name your price!"

The fat man's eyes widened. "*You* want it *back?*"

"It was stolen, Fritz," Andy said. "But not by The Chief."

Hummer was still looking at Jim Clay. "Stolen? From you, Mr. Clay? From your father's collection, maybe, eh? It must be very valuable. Well now, let's see, I paid a hundred dollars for it, and—"

"You paid twenty dollars!" Bob said angrily.

"So I lied a little." Fritz Hummer smiled nastily. "A man's entitled to a decent bit of profit, eh?"

"You'll get some profit," Jim Clay said. "Now, where is it?"

"In the back," Hummer said.

He led them back to a cluttered rear room—and stopped dead!

"It's gone!" Hummer cried. He pointed to a table near the back door. "It was right there!"

"The thief!" Jupiter exclaimed, and described the little man. "Did you see him anywhere around your shop?"

"Funny little guy with a cape?" Hummer said. "Come to think of it, there was a guy like that browsing in my shop earlier!"

Pete was at the rear door. "Jupe! This lock's broken!"

Jupiter examined the lock, then pushed on the door. It opened with a loud scraping. The alley was directly outside. Jupiter stood a moment, studying the door and the alley.

"I guess the thief got in from the alley, all right," Pete said unhappily. "While he had us locked in that boat."

"So it seems," Jupiter agreed.

"Fritz, could anyone come back into this room from the front without your noticing?" Andy asked.

"No one! You think I don't watch my customers? I've been robbed! A valuable statue!"

They returned to the front of the shop with the fat owner raging over his lost chance to make Jim Clay pay for the statue. Jupiter patted his pockets.

"I've dropped my pen," the stout leader said. "I'll be right back."

When he returned, they left Fritz Hummer still mumbling over his bad luck, and walked out into the late afternoon sun of the harbor. Andy, as usual, was taking things calmly, but Bob, Pete, and Jim Clay were disconsolate.

"It's gone!" Jim Clay said, his voice unbelieving.

"That thief must be miles away," said Bob. "He's probably headed for Mexico right now!"

"Perhaps," Jupiter said. "But if he is miles away, he doesn't have the statue!"

They all stared at him.

14

The Devil Knows!

"Hummer is lying," Jupiter declared. "I'm sure he knows where the statue is—and I'm sure the thief doesn't have it."

"How do you know that, Jupiter?" Jim demanded.

"The back door," Jupiter said. "The lock was broken, yes, but no one had opened that door for a long time before I did! It was so stiff I could barely get it open, and it scraped the ground all the way. It left a deep mark on the ground—the *only* mark. Pieces of rust broke off between the door and the frame. If it had been opened earlier, that rust would have been already broken off."

"Wow, Jupe's right!" Pete said. "I remember that rust!"

"Hummer knew that statue wasn't stolen! He just pretended it was and went along with us in blaming the thief! Remember how Hummer started to say he'd sold the statue—and then changed his story? I'm certain he suddenly realized that it might be very valuable. Did you see the greed in his eyes when you let him know it was part of your dad's collection?"

Jim was miserable. "I knew that was dumb right away."

"It was," Jupiter said severely. "Anyway, Hummer's sudden change of mind made me suspicious, the door proved no one could sneak in the back way, and this clinched it!" He held out a small lined page. "It's from some kind of account book. When Hummer took us in the back room, I saw him quickly close a notebook lying there. So I invented an excuse to go back there alone—and pulled this page out of the book. It says: 'Dancing statue, $100!' "

"He did sell it!" Bob fumed. "The liar!"

"But who'd he sell it to?" Jim cried. "We've got to make him tell us!"

"He'll tell us, Jim," Jupiter said. "Unless I'm very mistaken, now that he knows the Devil is worth much more than a hundred dollars, our greedy Mr. Hummer will try to get it back. All we have to do is wait and watch!"

"Jupe's right," Andy said, "and I bet it won't be long."

It wasn't. By the time Jim had gotten his station wagon and returned, the fat man had come out of his shop. He locked up, got into an old Ford, and drove off. In the Buick, the boys and their two friends followed.

Hummer stopped less than a mile away—at a Chinese laundry.

"Look!" Jim said as he drove slowly past the laundry. "There are statues in the window!"

"Just cheap imitations," Andy said. "Still—?"

Jim parked the Buick down the block and Pete walked

back to observe Hummer in the laundry. He almost ran into the fat man coming out of the store. As Pete slipped into the shadows of a doorway, the group in the Buick saw Hummer was carrying a package!

"Don't get excited!" said Pete when he returned to the car. "It's only his laundry."

Disappointed, Jim Clay slumped down in the driver's seat.

"Never mind," said Jupiter. "It's not surprising that he has chores to do."

Jim drove off after Hummer again. The fat man's next stop was in a shopping center across town, near the mountains. Hummer parked his car and went into a tavern. Andy volunteered to go in and see what he was doing.

"But he'll see you!" objected Pete.

"Maybe not," said Andy. "There seems to be a crowd in there. Anyway, he's used to seeing me around. He'd be more suspicious if he saw Jim. And you kids are too young to go in."

Guitar and all, the bearded young man went into the tavern. Five minutes later he came out again.

"Hummer is sitting at the bar having a sandwich and beer and talking to the barkeep," reported Andy. "Looks like he might be there awhile."

Jim Clay pounded his fist on the steering wheel. "He's got to lead us to the statue! He's *got* to!"

Andy announced he couldn't help them tail Hummer any more. "I promised some people to be somewhere now, so I've got to cut out."

The Investigators were disappointed, but Jim nodded and thanked Andy for his help.

"Yeah, well, good luck!" said Andy. "And remember what I told you, Pete," he added, winking at the Second Investigator. "Hang loose!"

Smiling, Andy sauntered off across the parking lot.

"Hang loose!" muttered Pete. "I'm too wound up to hang loose!"

Bob and Jupe laughed, and settled down to wait. Jim Clay didn't have the trained patience of the Investigators. He sighed repeatedly, and kept shifting his weight in the seat.

Hummer soon emerged from the tavern. Now the fat man's old Ford led them into the foothills to a big Victorian house up an overgrown canyon. While Pete stayed in the station wagon, Jupiter, Bob, and Jim crept through the weeds and brush up to the windows of the big turreted house. Through the living room window they saw Fritz Hummer talking to a very tall, pale man with a sharp nose and black hair. Dressed all in black, the tall man looked almost bloodless.

"Ulp," Bob whispered. "Good thing Pete's not here. That guy looks like a vampire!"

"Right out of *Dracula!*" agreed Jupe.

The tall man's black eyes were like empty holes in his pale face. He listened to Fritz Hummer, then motioned the fat man to follow him. They went into another room. The boys and Jim hurried along the side of the house to the windows of the room—but the shades were drawn!

They tried the other windows, but saw only empty rooms. There was nothing to do but return to the station wagon. Fritz Hummer came out only a few minutes later. He was still empty-handed, and drove off once more.

"He hasn't gotten any statue back yet," Pete observed as they drove after the old Ford.

"No," Jupiter said slowly, his voice uncertain now.

"You know," said Jim Clay, "I could swear I've seen that vampirelike man before."

"Yeah, in the movies!" said Bob.

"No. Somewhere in real life! But I just can't remember . . ." The young man fell silent and continued driving with an abstracted air.

Fritz Hummer led them right back to the harbor! The fat man returned to his shop, but instead of going into it climbed some stairs to the second story. A light went on in an upstairs window. Apparently the fat man lived over his shop.

"I guess that's it," Pete said. "No statue, First."

"No," Jupiter admitted mournfully. "I was so sure he would try to get it back at once . . ."

"Boys, maybe he did!" Jim Clay suddenly exclaimed. "I just remembered who that vampire man is! It's Jason Wilkes!"

"Who's that?" asked Pete.

"An art dealer! An unscrupulous art dealer! The Art Dealers Association threw him out for shady deals, and he's twice been accused of selling forgeries! He knows something about Oriental art—he's tried to do business with my dad! He came to our house once, but my dad told him to get lost!"

"Hmmm," said Jupe, his eyes gleaming. "Just the person to recognize a good piece among Fritz Hummer's junk—and not to ask questions about where it came from!"

"But Jupe," objected Pete, "if Jason Wilkes has the statue, how come Fritz Hummer didn't get it back from him?"

"Any number of reasons, Second. Possibly Wilkes refused to sell it back or had already sold it, or perhaps Hummer didn't want to be seen with it or didn't have enough cash."

"Or perhaps Wilkes never had it to begin with," Jim Clay added, suddenly glum. Then he brightened. "Maybe we saw Hummer arranging to get the statue to Wilkes, and he just hasn't gone to buy it back yet from whoever bought it."

"Oh, great!" said Pete. "Now what do we do?"

"Why can't we just ask Jason Wilkes if he's got the statue?" Bob wanted to know.

"No, no, that won't work," said Jim quickly. "At least, not until we're sure he has it. We don't want to get another person in on the act unnecessarily."

"I think we need a double stakeout," announced Jupiter. "Let's watch both Wilkes and Hummer and see what they do!"

"Just what I was thinking," said Jim. "But we'll have to split up. How can we keep in touch?"

"With our walkie-talkies!" said Bob. "We've got a bunch of them back at our headquarters!"

"We might have to follow somebody," said Jim, "and we might get out of range. We need a way to leave a trail."

"Well, there's always our chalk system," said Jupe. "We each take a piece of colored chalk and write question marks wherever we go. A question mark is quick to make, and few people notice them. "But," he added doubtfully, "the system's hard to use when you're in a car."

"It sounds fine to me," said Jim, brushing away objections. He cocked his ear at the window of the Buick. "Hear that? Hummer seems to have the ball game on upstairs. He's not going anywhere for a while. You kids are probably due home for dinner about now, right? I'll drive you home and pick up a walkie-talkie and some chalk. Then I'll come back here and watch Hummer. As soon as you can, you boys bike over to Wilkes's place and keep watch there. Report to me if anything happens, and I'll keep you posted on Hummer. Okay?"

"Yahoo!" cried Pete. "Dancing Devil, here we come!"

By sunset, The Three Investigators were in position in the bushes around Jason Wilkes's house. Pete and Jupiter were each on one side of the house, toward the front. Bob was stationed near the road, so he could warn if anyone approached the house.

Jupiter reported in to Jim Clay on his walkie-talkie:

"Nothing is happening here, Jim. There's a car in the garage out back and a light on upstairs, but we haven't seen any movement."

"Nothing's happening here either," Jim's voice whispered across the distance. "Hummer has the TV on—I can see the flickers. He's still watching the ball game. I've got it on the car radio—it's a doubleheader. Second game just started."

"Could be a long night," commented Jupiter. "I'll check with you every half hour."

The Investigators began their vigil. The sky grew darker, until there was only the faint light of stars and a waning moon to see by. No lights showed along the road—Jason Wilkes had no near neighbors. The canyon beyond the house loomed darkly. Periodically Jupe and Pete crept along the house and looked in all the unshaded windows. They saw nothing. No one moved inside.

"Car coming!" Bob's voice came softly to the others after an hour.

The Investigators tensed for action. The car drove slowly past the lonely house and then stopped where the road came to a dead end, a short way up the canyon. But no one got out. A moment later the car turned around and went back down the road.

"False alarm," said Bob. "Somebody took the wrong way, I guess."

More time passed. Jim reported that the ball game was over, but Hummer hadn't budged from his apartment. It was getting late, and the double vigil was proving fruitless. Then Pete reported, stammering, from the far side of the house:

"Fe–fe–fellows! Something's moving over here! I can't see . . . Wait . . . *Ulp!* It's the thing! The Dancing Devil! I can see the head!"

Silence!

"Pete?" Jupiter cried softly into his walkie-talkie as he ran toward Pete's station. "I'm coming."

"Second?" Bob said anxiously from the road.

Jim's voice came faintly: "Is Pete all right?"

"It's gone!" Pete's excited voice came again. "Fellows, it was looking in the window, then it went off up the canyon! You think it knows the statue's here?"

"I'm sure of it!" Jim said. "Hang in there, boys. I'm coming!"

15

Victory–And Defeat!

"It's . . . it's gone, fellows," Pete said shakily.

Jupiter and Bob had slipped through the thick brush to where Pete crouched, his face ghostly in the faint moonlight.

"Careful," Jupiter warned. "That Dancing Devil could be anywhere."

Silent outside the big, shadowy house, they searched the night with nervous eyes.

"Where did you see it last, Second?" Jupiter asked.

"Right next to the house. Then it seemed to vanish up the canyon—or somewhere beyond the house, anyway."

"Where did it come from, Pete?" Bob wanted to know.

"I . . . I don't know. It just appeared. Right at the side of the house. Almost like . . . like . . ."

"Like it came right out of the wall? Through the wall?" Bob said. "Like a . . . spirit?"

"You said it," Pete said. "I didn't!"

Bob looked toward the dark, silent house. "Jupe? You think Jason Wilkes could *be* the Dancing Devil?"

"The thought has occurred to me, Records," Jupiter admitted.

"But why, First?" Pete wondered. "If he has the statue?"

"Perhaps precisely *because* he has it, Second," Jupiter analyzed. "To scare everyone away so that they won't trace the statue to him. He's an art dealer—he must know what the statue really is and how valuable it is. Perhaps that thief was taking the statue to Wilkes when he lost it, and Wilkes has been trying to scare us off ever since!"

The Investigators waited in the darkness, but there was no further sign of the Devil. Then, in a group, they cautiously circled the house. Nothing moved—inside or out.

A few minutes later Jim Clay arrived. He parked his station wagon down the road and walked slowly toward the house.

"Jupe? Pete? Bob?" Jim called softly.

"Over here," Jupiter whispered from some bushes by the road. He filled Jim in on what had happened, and offered his new theory that Jason Wilkes was the Dancing Devil.

Jim Clay studied the dark house. His eyes gleamed restlessly.

"Jupiter? If Wilkes is the Dancing Devil, and he's gone somewhere, then the house must be empty," the youth said. "Have you seen anyone in there since the Devil appeared?"

"No," Pete said, "but we didn't see anyone in there even before. The whole place seems empty—even when the Devil is around."

"Now who's seeing spirits!" Bob said.

"I think," Jupiter said, "that our Dancing Devil is real, alive, and quite human. In fact, I'm sure of it."

"I wish I was," Jim Clay said, "and I haven't even seen it! But the way you guys describe him, he's exactly like the statue, and my dad says the Mongols believe there's a spirit in all things!"

"We know," Pete groaned.

"Well," Jim went on, "real or spirit, it's gone now. What do you think we should do, Jupiter?"

Jupiter nodded in the night. "The same as you, Jim. We should try to get in and search the house!"

"Go in?" Pete cried, muffling his voice.

"It may be our last chance, Second," Jupiter said.

"Gosh, Jupe," Bob said, "maybe we ought to get Chief Reynolds first."

"That could be too late, Bob," Jim said. "And we don't know the statue's in there for sure. I know that my dad wouldn't want the police if we could get it back quietly."

"Well," Pete decided, "as long as that Dancing Devil's gone, I guess it's worth a try. But I'll keep watch."

"That's a good idea," Jupiter agreed. "If you see anyone, sing out."

"You'd hear me if you were in New York!"

The other three moved off toward the dark house. Jim quickly found a window open, and they climbed in silently. As their eyes became accustomed to the gloom, they saw that they were in a room almost as large as Jim's father's Collection Room, and just as crowded with glass cases, cupboards, and shadowy objects.

"Jupe!" Bob whispered, suddenly scared. "There!"

The grotesque lionlike face seemed to glare down at them from a ghostly human body! Jupiter and Bob turned to flee, but Jim Clay stood his ground and peered at the figure.

"It's a big statue, fellows," he said slowly. "A Tibetan temple guardian. Only a fake, I think."

Bob and Jupiter calmed down and took out the tiny pencil flashlights they'd brought with them. Flicking them on, they moved through the room with Jim. It was Jupiter who saw the second figure towering in the shadows.

"Wha . . . what's that!" the stout boy gasped.

A capering shape with four arms, a high crown, and a circle of disembodied hands!

"It's Siva," Jim declared softly. "A Hindu god. Another fake!"

Jupiter looked up at the statue in the dimness. "Siva? The Indian god? I thought you said you didn't know anything about Oriental art."

"I guess I know more than I thought," Jim whispered with a grin. "My dad's always talking about art. I suppose a lot rubbed off."

"Maybe he can rub some off on me," Jupiter whispered back. "I'd like to know a lot more than I do about it all."

"Well," Jim said, "when he gets back, I'll—"

Across the shadowy room, Bob turned.

"Jim?" the Records man of the team called softly. "Is this a fake, too?"

Jim and Jupiter walked through the messy room to Bob. He was holding a small green statue with a shaggy, horned head!

"It's the Dancing Devil!" Jim cried, forgetting for the moment to whisper. "You've got it, Bob!"

"Shhhhhhhh!" Jupiter hissed.

Jim froze, and the three of them stood listening. There was no sound anywhere, and nothing moved. Reassured, they crowded around the small statue. Both penlights illuminated it.

"Wow!" Bob exclaimed softly. "It's exactly like the live Devil!"

Green with age, the bronze statue was clear and exact in every detail. The spreading yak horns were smooth and sharp. Every hair showed on the shaggy mask with its slit eyes and gaping, toothed mouth. The wolf head hanging in front looked real enough to bite them! On the legs and arms, lifted in dance, the padding almost felt soft.

"Look at the belt," Bob said quietly. "The bells even have tiny clappers, and the roots have dirt on them. That ear of corn isn't half an inch long, but I can see the kernels!"

"We've got it!" Jim enthused.

"You're sure it's the real Dancing Devil?" Jupiter said. "It's pretty clean for something so old."

"Of course I'm sure!" Jim declared. "I've seen it lots of times before. There's only one like it in the world, and we've got it back! Come on, guys, my dad'll reward you for this!"

Bob and Jupiter stood staring at the dancing figure of the Mongol shaman for another moment. They'd been looking for it for so long, and now they had found it! They grinned at each other as Bob tucked the statue under his arm and turned to follow Jim out.

Jim wasn't going out! The tycoon's son was standing and looking at the door of the room. Someone was coming!

"Pete!" Jupiter and Bob said together.

The Second Investigator walked into the room.

"We've got the Dancing Devil, Pete!" Bob crowed, grinning.

A thin voice behind Pete said, "Do you, boy? I think not."

"I . . . I'm sorry, fellows," Pete said miserably. "He got me from behind. I . . . I didn't hear him."

Light flashed on in the room. The pale-faced, black-eyed Jason Wilkes came in behind Pete. He had a gun in his skeletal hand.

"Give the statue to me, boy!" he said coldly.

Reluctantly, Bob handed over the Dancing Devil. Wilkes looked at it fondly and put it down.

"I confiscated this"—Wilkes held up a walkie-talkie—"from your confederate. The rest of you will kindly drop your instruments on the floor."

Jim, Bob, and Jupiter slowly pulled out their walkie-talkies and dropped them. Bob and Jupe hastily pocketed their pencil flashlights. Jason Wilkes didn't seem to notice, or perhaps he didn't care.

"You will all walk ahead of me to the rear of the house."

They walked slowly back through the house. Wilkes flicked on lights along the way. He stopped them at a heavy door off the kitchen.

"Open it, and go down."

Pete opened the door, and they saw narrow wooden stairs going down into total blackness.

"You will remain with me, Mr. Clay," Wilkes said. "A

small insurance, eh? For an added incentive in my dealings with your esteemed father—or whoever may offer more for the statue."

Wilkes laughed thinly. Jim Clay looked helplessly at the boys as they started down the steps. Before they were half-way down, the heavy door slammed shut!

16

Bob Saves the Day

"We've lost the Dancing Devil again!" Bob wailed as they stood in darkness on the narrow stairs. "He's got it, and Jim, too!"

"I should have spotted him out there," Pete castigated himself. "But he was on me before I even heard him! He must have been watching us all the time! He knew right where I was."

"We'll never stop him now," Bob said with despair.

"This is no time to give up, Records!" Jupiter said sternly. "We must get out of here. Shine your penlight back up at the top of the stairs and see if there's a light switch up there," he instructed.

Bob pointed his light upward. He played the beam everywhere at the top of the narrow stairs. There was no light switch.

"Maybe it's down at the bottom," Pete said.

They continued slowly down by the narrow beams of their penlights until they reached a hard dirt floor. There was no switch at the bottom of the stairs, either.

"It's an old cellar," Jupiter observed. "Perhaps there's a pull cord on the light."

Each of the boys turned his penlight on a different part of the low ceiling. Not only was there no pull cord, there wasn't even a bulb in the single overhead fixture. Pete slumped down on a dusty crate.

"We're stuck in the dark," he said, dejected.

"And nobody even knows we're here!" Bob added gloomily.

"Jason Wilkes will probably let us out sometime," Jupiter said. "*After* he's sold the statue! Then we'll have no evidence against him. It will be too late to do us any good. We must get out now!"

From where he sat on the rickety crate, Pete played his penlight slowly all around the low, dark cellar.

"How, Jupe?" he asked.

The narrow beam of his small light picked out the dank dirt floor and the heavy beams of the low ceiling. The stone-walled cellar was almost completely bare, with no furniture, no workshop, and no tools. The boys saw only the narrow stairs going up to the kitchen door, one other low door on the far side, two narrow little windows high up, laundry sinks, a row of bins, and an old gravity furnace, small and rusty in the center of the dirt floor.

"There's always a way, Second! We've proven that before," Jupiter insisted stoutly. "That low door! Unless I'm very wrong, it's an outside entrance to this cellar."

The portly leader of the trio crossed to the small door. Pete and Bob shone their lights on it. There was no lock, but the door was barred from inside, and nailed to its frame. Pete shook his head.

"There must be twenty-five big nails in that door," the Second Investigator said, "and we don't have anything to get them out with."

"Besides," Bob said, standing back and looking along the stone wall where the door was set. "I think we looked pretty closely at this wall outside, and I don't remember any outside entrance, First. I'll bet it's totally blocked up."

"The windows, then!" Jupiter said.

He recrossed the dark cellar with a firm step and looked up at the two narrow windows set just below the ceiling. In the beam of his penlight the windows were dark, but held shut by only an ordinary latch!

"Second! Records! Bring that box! The windows aren't locked!"

Pete carried the dusty box to the nearest window, and Bob climbed up on it. Eagerly, he unlatched the small window, swung it up to where it hooked onto the ceiling, and . . .

"Bars!" Bob cried, deflated. "They've got bars on the outside!"

The silence hung heavy in the dark cellar. Even Jupiter slumped in discouragement as Bob climbed down and stood looking disconsolately at the barred window. But the rotund First Investigator was not a boy who gave up easily.

"All right, sometimes storage bins have chutes from the outside," he said. "Or maybe we'll find some old tools, something to get out those nails in the door."

Pete sat down on the box again. "You look, First, I don't want to discover any more bad news."

Bob joined Jupiter in a penlight inspection of the low bins built against one wall. Their wood was decaying, and they were all empty except for spider webs. The stone wall at the back of the bins was smooth and without holes or chutes.

"I guess it's useless, First," Bob said at last. "We're just stuck down here until Wilkes decides to let us out—if he ever does."

He went to join Pete under the window, and sat on the dirt with his back against the wall. Jupiter stood alone in his own small circle of light.

"At least the window's open," he said. "We can be heard clearly outside when we shout. We'll take turns yelling, five minutes every fifteen minutes."

"Jupe, this house is all alone up the canyon," Bob pointed out glumly. "There's no one around to hear us."

"Except maybe the Dancing Devil!" Pete said.

Even the vigorous Jupiter couldn't go on forever in the face of hopelessness. He sighed and sat down on the bottom of the stairs, stabbing at the dirt floor with his toe. His eyes flashed as if in a last, brief flare.

"The floor's dirt," he said. "Maybe we can dig our way out."

Pete nodded. "Sure, First. With just our hands. It won't take more than a week or so."

Jupiter sighed.

"Fellows," Bob said, "the furnace. Look at that duct."

The rusty old gravity furnace was in the exact center of the low cellar. Two large and three small round ducts radiated from it. The large ducts were at least big enough for a boy to crawl through. Jupiter nodded, and sighed again.

"I thought of that at once, Records. But gravity-furnace ducts go up to heavy floor registers. They're as good as bars."

"Sure—if they run only up into the house," Bob said. He stood up in the dark cellar. "But this is a California half cellar, First! Look at its width—it's only under about half the house. There's probably a crawlway under the rest of the house. That big duct runs outside before turning up into the house!"

"He's right, First!" Pete yelped.

The three boys quickly pulled the rusty lightweight pipe from the wall, revealing a hole large enough for boys to crawl through. Most boys, anyway.

"I'll see where it goes," Bob said.

The smallest of the boys, Bob disappeared into the black opening. On tiptoe, Pete watched the tiny glow of the pen-light bobbing along the dark duct. Bob reached the elbow joint where the duct turned upwards. There was a tearing of sheet metal. Bob's muffled voice came back:

"There *is* a crawlway! I'm under the house. Come on!"

Pete offered to help Jupiter up into the duct. The stout leader's face reddened.

"You and Bob crawl out, Second, and open the door for me."

Pete grinned, and crawled away along the duct to join Bob under the house. Together they crawled to the edge of the building. Screens covered the opening between the house and the ground. They pushed out a screen and snaked through into the open air.

"P–Pete?" Bob whispered.

A pair of legs stood in front of them! They both looked up—into a pair of black, cold Oriental eyes!

17

On the Trail of a Villain

Short and heavy, the man wore a high-collared dark-blue jacket that showed no shirt or tie, straight dark-blue trousers with no crease, and an angry look in his eyes. Behind him in the dark night were two more men.

One of them was the assistant, Walter Quail! The black Mercedes he'd been driving around town was parked on the road.

"So?" the Oriental man said harshly. "Where is the Dancing Devil?"

Bob and Pete stood up slowly, brushing the dirt from their trousers.

"We . . . we don't know," Bob admitted. "Wilkes took—"

The third man strode forward, brusquely elbowed the Oriental man aside, and glared at the two boys.

"Did you say Wilkes, young man? You mean—Jason Wilkes?"

He was a big, bluff man with a strong face, iron-gray hair, and the shoulders of a football player. His expensive suit was a sharp contrast to the drab garb of the Oriental man.

"That's right, sir. The art dealer," Pete said. "He got the Dancing Devil from Fritz Hummer, who got it from The Chief, who—"

"Hummer? Chief? What in tarnation is going on?" the big man thundered. "Do you know who I am, young fellow?"

Bob said, "You're H. P. Clay! The oil tycoon."

"Tycoon, is it?" H. P. Clay laughed. "Just a businessman, son." Jim's father nodded to the Oriental man. "This is Special Envoy Chiang Pi-Peng of the People's Republic of China, who's come to accept the Dancing Devil for his government. I understand you already know Quail there."

"Yes, sir," Bob said. "I'm Bob Andrews, this is Pete Crenshaw, and our partner is still locked in the house, sir. If—"

"Locked in?" Mr. Clay said. "Well, let's get him out."

They trooped into the old house. Jupiter blinked owlishly at Chiang Pi-Peng and Mr. Clay as they let him out of the cellar, and narrowed his eyes as he saw Walter Quail. The bespectacled assistant shifted uneasily under Jupiter's scrutiny.

"You have to be Jupiter Jones, then," Mr. Clay boomed. "An unlikely name if I ever heard one, but maybe you can tell me just what's been going on?"

Without going into detail, Jupiter described the Investigators' and Jim's efforts to recover the missing statue.

"Jim was quite right, it's a devilishly touchy matter. The fewer who know about it the better. Now—" The big businessman stopped, and looked around. "Where is Jim? Isn't he with you?"

"No, sir," Jupiter said, and told the big tycoon what had happened earlier that night.

"You mean that skunk Jason Wilkes has Jim a prisoner? Jim and the Dancing Devil!" Mr. Clay went pale. He turned to his assistant. "Didn't you tell me that Jim said he was here in this house with these boys?"

Walter Quail nodded, his eye twitching nervously. "Yes, sir, he described the place, where it was, and said he was calling from here. He—"

"He called you?" Jupiter said. "You mean tonight? That's how you knew we were here?"

"He called about an hour ago," Walter Quail explained. "Just as I was leaving to pick up Mr. Clay and Mr. Chiang at the airport. I thought I should get them first. We came straight here."

"Never mind all that!" H. P. Clay thundered. "Exactly what did Jim say when he called you, Walter? Every word!"

"Yes," Jupiter agreed. "Perhaps there's a clue as to where he could be!"

"Well." Quail knitted his brows behind the rimless glasses. "I was about to leave for the airport when Stevens said James was on the telephone and sounded urgent. When I took the call, he sounded extremely agitated, and said he had to talk fast. He said he and the boys were trapped in this house, and told me where it was. Then he said he'd found the Dancing Devil and lost it again. He was about to name his captor when the phone went dead."

"Gosh," Pete said, "he must have gotten away from Wilkes for a moment and made the call."

"More likely Wilkes had him locked in a room here, and forgot there was a telephone in it," Bob said.

"Whatever," Mr. Clay said, pacing the floor, "none of that tells us a thing! We're stymied! That Wilkes has all the cards."

Chiang Pi-Peng said quietly in perfect English, "Your son is in danger, Mr. Clay? And this man also has the Dancing Devil?"

"He's got the Devil all right, Mr. Chiang," H. P. Clay said grimly, continuing to pace. "I don't think Jim is in any immediate danger, though. This Wilkes undoubtedly wants to sell the Devil back to me, at an exorbitant price I'm sure, and poor Jim is a hostage to keep me honest."

"Sir?" Jupiter said. "There is one more thing," and he told the tycoon about the apparition that had been pursuing them.

"A live Dancing Devil? That's impossible!" Mr. Clay cried.

"Or a spirit," Bob said. "The spirit of the statue."

"Reactionary nonsense!" Mr. Chiang said, but the Chinese politician wiped his brow nervously. "Mongol superstition! The myths of a backward people whom we must save from their own ignorance. There are no spirits!"

His voice was clear and firm, but he looked around in the silent house as if watching the shadows.

"A real shaman, then," Jupiter said. "Or perhaps someone who wants us to think he's a real shaman."

"Real or fake," Mr. Clay snapped, "stymied or not, I'm not going to just give up! Everyone search for a clue. Two of you boys can search the house with me. One of you go with Quail and Mr. Chiang and search the grounds outside."

Bob and Pete went with Mr. Clay and searched the old house from top to bottom. Jupiter joined Chiang and Quail and went outside.

It was close to midnight when Mr. Clay, Bob, and Pete gave up and went out to join the others. They had found nothing in the house that gave any indication of where Jason Wilkes and Jim could be. Neither Mr. Chiang nor Quail had anything to report from their search of the grounds around the house.

"I'm afraid that's it. We'll just have to go home and wait," Mr. Clay said wearily. "They could be anywhere."

Jupiter came out of the garage. "I think not, sir. Jason Wilkes's car is still in the garage—I checked the registration and it's his. I see no evidence of another car, and I saw Jim's Estate Wagon still parked down the road. That means that wherever they are, they must have walked! We'll spread out and search in every direction!"

Bob and Quail searched down the road on both sides. Mr. Chiang and Jupiter took the rear of the grounds, and Mr. Clay and Pete went up the road, farther into the dark canyon. They moved in a slowly widening circle away from the old house.

"First!" Pete cried. "Records!"

Through the night they all converged on Pete. He stood some hundred yards up the dark, narrow canyon beyond the old house. The tall boy pointed with his penlight to a large rock, and then ahead to a broken fence board.

"Jim remembered our chalk trail!" Bob exclaimed.

Chalked question marks glowed dimly on the flat rock and on the fence board, pointing like an arrow up the canyon.

18 ════════════════════════════

The Dancing Devil Strikes!

"Find the next question mark!" Jupiter urged.

Bob found it on a tree some twenty yards deeper into the dark canyon.

"There's no doubt, then!" Jupiter exclaimed. "Wilkes must have taken Jim and the statue somewhere up this canyon."

"How can you be so sure?" wondered Mr. Clay.

"The question marks are the secret signal we use to lay a trail for someone to follow," Pete said.

"They can be made quickly, without attracting the notice of a captor," Jupiter added.

"And we gave Jim some chalk and told him how to leave the trail if we got separated," Bob finished.

"Then what are we standing here for?" Mr. Clay demanded. "Let's find my son!"

Pete took the lead as the best tracker, with Mr. Clay close behind him. The others followed in single file, with Quail and Mr. Chiang bringing up the rear. Pete spotted the fourth and fifth question marks on rocks. The trail was leading straight back into the canyon.

"What's back in here?" Mr. Clay wanted to know.

"Probably not much—there's not even a road here any more," Bob pointed out. "We might find an old abandoned farmhouse or some empty prospectors' shacks. I'm sure no one lives up this canyon."

The question marks continued deeper and deeper into the narrowing canyon. The land grew rockier, steeper, and rougher, with the side walls rising higher into the night and the thorny chaparral tearing at their clothing. The moon had set, and the group had only the tiny beams of the Investigators' penlights to see by. They stumbled and slid over the rugged ground, and then the trail vanished!

"Where's the next mark?" Mr. Clay cried anxiously.

"Spread out and look," Jupiter said, "but keep in sight or calling distance of the man next to you. It's easy to lose your way out here at night."

It took twenty minutes for Mr. Chiang to find the next question mark a hundred yards ahead and to the right.

"Wilkes must have decided to zigzag a little to confuse his trail through the brush," Pete said. "Look for the next mark back to the left."

They found it, and went on—but more slowly now as the marks were farther apart and in a zigzag pattern. Wilkes had been cautious, but the marks were still there leading up the canyon, so he hadn't discovered what Jim was doing!

They were half a mile in, the sides of the canyon quite high now, when Walter Quail cried out.

"Ahhhh—ohhhhh—!"

They all turned quickly. Last in the line, Walter Quail sat on the rocky ground. He held his left ankle.

"I think I've sprained it," he said, gritting his teeth. "That rock turned under me. I'm sorry, Mr. Clay."

"Can you walk at all?" H. P. Clay asked.

"Yes, but I'd hold you back. You must go ahead. James may need help!"

Mr. Clay hesitated for only a moment. "All right, Walter. Follow along as fast as you can."

The rest of them pushed on into the wilderness, with Mr. Chiang bringing up the rear now. They stepped more carefully as the ground grew rockier and the chaparral more dense. The narrow canyon turned sharply left, and suddenly widened again just as they lost the trail of question marks a second time.

"All right," Pete said. "Spread out again, and move ahead real slow until we spot—"

The indistinct figure appeared directly ahead up the canyon, coming straight toward them.

"Jim?" Mr. Clay cried out.

The dark figure stopped as if slapped. It stood there in the night, motionless and making no sound.

"Is that you, Jim?" Mr. Clay called again.

The vague figure began to walk toward the right side of the canyon. The Investigators shone their penlights on the shape, lighting a pale face, black hair, and all black clothes. A small sack dangled from one hand. The man began to run.

"It's Jason Wilkes!" Jupiter exclaimed.

"He's carrying something!" Pete cried.

"Stop him!" Mr. Clay shouted.

Jason Wilkes ran toward the side of the steep canyon. His pursuers raced at an angle to cut him off.

Then Wilkes vanished!

Stumbling and careening through the darkness and the thick chaparral on the steep slope, the five pursuers peered ahead to where the fleeing man had disappeared.

"There's an opening!" Bob pointed out.

"A side canyon!" Pete cried.

They burst through the narrow opening, clogged with twisted live oaks, and came out into a small box canyon with high, craggy sides—and no other way out!

They stopped.

Ahead, Jason Wilkes stood under the high wall of the box canyon. His black eyes glowed like the eyes of some cornered animal. He was trapped.

"What have you done with my son, you scoundrel!" Mr. Clay demanded.

The vampirelike art dealer looked left and right as if searching for some way out. They walked slowly toward him, the flashlights of the boys pinning him against the canyon wall like a great, black insect. A stinging insect, whose black eyes still shot fire.

"Keep away, or you may never know!" Wilkes snarled. "I was about to contact you, but maybe you've saved me the trouble."

"I don't deal with kidnappers!" Mr. Clay raged.

Wilkes laughed. "Your son and those stupid kids there

broke into my house. I am simply holding your son until I can turn him over to the police. I'm within my rights, Mr. Clay. I'll have your son arrested—unless we can make a fair deal."

Pete exclaimed, "That sack! I'll bet he's got the statue!"

"You have my property! Stolen property!" Clay said.

Wilkes smiled now. "I didn't know that. Let's call it a stand-off, easily settled with a modest payment on your part."

Mr. Chiang was staring at the sack in Jason Wilkes's hand. "He has in that sack the Dancing Devil? Then we must agree—"

The flash of dazzling light seemed to fill the box canyon!

A blinding flash that made them all stagger back, their hands up covering their eyes!

A pillar of smoke rose high on the cliff behind Jason Wilkes!

"Aaaaahhhhhhhhhrrrrrrrrrrr—!"

Its horns spreading, its red eyes glowing in their slits, the apparition of the Dancing Devil stood on the rocky wall above the canyon. It moved slowly as if in a trance, its bells and bones jangling through the dark night.

The hollow voice boomed out across the small canyon:

"The Dancing Devil of Batu Khan is defiled!"

Trembling, Jason Wilkes dropped his sack and stumbled back toward the boys, Mr. Clay, and Chiang Pi-Peng. He stared in terror at the apparition on the cliff.

"Keep it away from me!" he moaned. "Keep it back!"

Mr. Clay was pale, but he stood his ground. "Whatever you are, you don't scare—"

"*Silence!*" The hollow voice boomed. "*The defiled shell must be destroyed! The spirit must be freed!*"

The shaggy apparition raised its arms wide above its horned head, then swept its right arm down to point straight at the sack that lay on the ground. A flash, a puff of thick smoke, and the sack burst into flames!

"*The spirit returns to the Great Khan!*"

Another flash of flame showed high on the cliff. A thick pillar of smoke engulfed the barbaric shape and slowly drifted away in the night.

The Dancing Devil was gone.

19

The Face at the Window

On the cliff above, there was only drifting smoke.

"He's . . . it's . . . gone!" Pete stammered.

"Only . . . smoke," Bob said, awestruck.

"Nonsense!" H. P. Clay declared. "It's some kind of trick!"

Chiang Pi-Peng stood transfixed, staring upward at the smoke still hanging in the night. His voice was low and strange.

"The spirits? Could it be true?" the Chinese man said.

H. P. Clay snorted. "A trick, nothing more! Some kind of projected image and a loudspeaker. Flares and smoke bombs. All an illusion. Probably all the work of Wilkes there!"

The tycoon turned on Jason Wilkes, who cringed away.

"You'd better confess, Wilkes! Where is my son and the

Dancing Devil?"

"Fellows! Mr. Clay!"

It was Pete. The Second Investigator stood over the smoldering remnants of the sack that Jason Wilkes had dropped.

"If it was all an illusion, I sure hope this is some illusion too," he said, pushing the charred cloth away with his foot to reveal a small, heavy object.

They all looked down at the shapeless mass of metal.

"It's the statue!" Bob exclaimed.

"It *was* the statue," Pete corrected him.

"Destroyed!" Mr. Clay cried, his face white.

"Melted!" Mr. Chiang said in horror. "Gone forever!"

Jupiter knelt down and brushed away the rest of the charred cloth of the sack. He touched the twisted mass of metal.

"It's barely warm," he said, his voice low in a kind of wonder. "The burning sack wasn't hot enough to melt bronze."

"Something melted it," Pete said.

They looked at each other in silence. Chiang Pi-Peng finally spoke:

"That . . . spirit . . . apparition," he said uneasily. "It said the statue had to be destroyed. In the name of Batu, grandson of Genghis, and Khan of the Golden Horde!"

Once more they were all silent.

"You're sure it's the statue of the Dancing Devil, Jupiter?" Mr. Clay asked in a choked voice.

Jupiter nodded. "I can see one horn, and the leg on what's left of the pedestal. Part of the middle isn't melted, I can make out the single ear of corn on the belt that—" He stopped, blinked, and then peered closely at the lump of melted bronze.

"Gone then! Gone!" Jason Wilkes suddenly moaned. "Priceless, and I had it! A fortune in my hands!"

"After more than seven hundred years—gone," Mr. Chiang said, and turned away.

"All right, it's gone," Mr. Clay said, his voice strong again. "We can't bring it back. But my son is still missing! Wilkes—!"

"He's okay," Jason Wilkes said, his voice surly. "It doesn't matter now. I'll take you to him. Remember, he was a burglar in my house! I had a right to hold him."

"We'll see what the police have to say about that, you scoundrel!" Mr. Clay said. "Now take us!"

With the tycoon walking close behind Jason Wilkes, they all filed out of the box canyon back into the main canyon. Prodded by Clay, Wilkes turned up the canyon and headed deeper into the mountains. Suddenly Bob raised his hand.

"Over there! What's that?" Bob pointed in the night.

A darker shadow lay on the ground in a clearing in the chaparral. Even as they reached it, the shape began to moan. Holding his head, Walter Quail sat up on the ground.

"Quail!" Mr. Clay cried. "What happened?"

"I was following you along as fast as I could," the assistant said weakly. "I got to about here, and then I didn't hear you ahead of me any more. I listened, and thought I heard you all off to the right. As I started that way, I sensed something on top of me. Before I could turn, or see anything, I was hit. That's the last I remember until just now when I heard you coming back this way."

The thin assistant touched his head and winced. His rimless glasses were hanging down in front on their black ribbon. His prim suit was dirty and leaf-covered. He brushed at it, grimacing as if the movement hurt his head.

"You didn't see who hit you?" Jupiter asked.

"I'm afraid not," Quail said. "I neither saw nor heard a thing. I just had a sense of *something* there, and then I was hit."

"Spirits are not seen or heard," Chiang Pi-Peng said, "until they wish to be."

"Spirits?" Quail said nervously.

Mr. Clay told him about what had happened in the box canyon.

"The statue is destroyed?" the assistant cried, and bit his lip. "And you think that . . . thing hit me?"

"Probably," H. P. Clay said. "But that's water under the bridge. We must release Jim. Can you walk with us?"

"I'll try," Quail said.

They helped him up, and, limping, he followed along as Mr. Clay pushed Jason Wilkes on up the canyon. Wilkes noticed the trail of question marks chalked in the night.

"So that's how you tailed me," he said bitterly.

"Jim and the boys were too smart for you," Mr. Clay said.

Then they came around another turn in the canyon. Ahead, across a clearing, a small shack loomed.

"He's in there," Jason Wilkes said. "I didn't touch him— just held him a while."

Mr. Clay hurried to the shack. The door was barred and bolted from the outside. Pete and Bob helped the tycoon tear off the bar and bolts and swing open the light door. They shone their penlights inside.

"You . . . leave . . . me . . . alone!" a shaky voice said, scared but defiant.

Jim Clay sat huddled in a corner of the small two-room shack, his knees drawn up to his chin, and his eyes wide and furtive like some frightened animal's. But there was fire in the eyes, too. The tall youth struggled up, a narrow board in his hand, ready to resist.

"Jim, boy!" Mr. Clay cried, walking forward.

"Dad?" Jim said, blinking in the light after so long in the dark shack. "Pete! Bob! You've got that skunk!"

"We've got him," Mr. Clay said, gripping his son's shoulder.

"We followed your trail!" Bob grinned.

"Gee, I hoped you'd spot it. I was beginning to give up hope after Wilkes left me locked in here, and took the Dancing Devil away . . . The statue! You got that, too?"

Mr. Clay shook his head. "No, son, I'm afraid that it's gone for good."

"That . . . thing, the apparition, destroyed it," Bob said.

"It was all melted, ruined," Pete added.

Mr. Chiang's voice was like a singsong chant. "The Dancing Devil has returned its spirit to Batu, Khan of the Golden Horde."

"You . . . you mean that *thing* was real? A spirit shaman? And it destroyed the statue to free its spirit?" Jim said.

"Well, Jupiter thinks—" Bob began, and he stopped. He looked all around in the dim shack. "Where's Jupe?"

Pete whirled, searching with his eyes.

"Why," Mr. Clay said, "he's not here! He—"

"The window!" Walter Quail cried. "Look!"

Bob and Pete shone their penlights at the window in the rear wall.

The shaggy, horned head with the red slit-eyes and gaping mouth peered in at them all!

"It's come back!" Mr. Clay cried.

Then the barbaric head seemed to rise into the air, and in its place the round face of Jupiter was framed in the dark window.

"No, it's not back," the First Investigator said from outside.

He disappeared, and they could hear him coming around the shack. They all looked toward the door. The stout leader of the detective trio came into the shack carrying the shaggy head with its spreading yak horns, and the apparition's belt with all the bells and rattles and roots on it.

"It's not back because it never really existed," he announced. "And the Dancing Devil hasn't been destroyed!"

20

The Devil Unmasked!

"What are you talking about, Jupiter?" Mr. Clay demanded. "Where did you find that mask?"

"I found it in the chaparral out behind this shack, sir," Jupiter said, coming slowly into the dim room. "The rest of the costume is there too, including the tiny red lights and battery used to make the eyes glow, and some of the chemicals that made the smoke and flashes of flame. Most ingenious, but not difficult for someone with knowledge of chemistry."

He looked at Mr. Clay. "I believe, if you inspect the mask and other parts of the costume, sir, you'll find that they come from your collection."

Mr. Clay scowled. "Well, I think I have some masks like that in my storage vault, yes. I have a lot of Mongol items down there I haven't classified or displayed yet. But what made you look out back?"

"I never believed that the apparition was a real spirit, and after I realized the big trick played on us, a lot of small things added up. For a time I thought there could be a real Mongol shaman after the Dancing Devil, but when Mr. Chiang came I discarded that idea. Mr. Clay was returning the statue, so why would a real shaman come for it?" The stout First Investigator shook his head. "No, the apparition had to be something else, so I followed a hunch and looked out in back here."

Pete was almost bursting. "What big trick was played on us, Jupe?"

"The trick of destroying the statue, Second. The Dancing Devil wasn't destroyed out there in the canyon."

Mr. Chiang shook his head. "We all saw it destroyed, young man. You yourself saw—"

"We saw *a* statue destroyed," Jupiter said. "We didn't see *the* statue destroyed. We've never seen the real Dancing Devil, but only a fake all along!"

"Fake?" Bob said doubtfully. "Jupe, you're no expert in—"

"Gosh, Jupiter," Jim said. "You can't be sure of that. I don't think even I could be."

H. P. Clay's eyes were narrow. "Can you be sure, Jupiter?"

"Oh, yes, I'm very sure. It's a replica that was melted, I know that. A very good replica. Made, I expect, by that little thief in the cape. He never did look like a thief, did he, Pete?"

"No," Pete said. "I remember we wondered about that."

"I expect we'll find he's an artist, if not very honest," Jupiter said. "He made the replica, brought it to Rocky Beach, and then lost it! And that's how we got into it all."

"How can you be sure, Jupiter?" Jim wondered. "When we found it, it looked exactly the same as always to me."

Jupiter nodded. "It was a fine replica, but I think the artist made it from photographs only. He didn't copy from the actual statue, probably because he couldn't get at it without raising suspicion, and the pictures he used didn't show all the details clearly. So he made a mistake!"

"Mistake?" Mr. Clay snapped.

"Yes, sir," Jupiter said, and his eyes gleamed. "He couldn't make out the tiny details of the objects on the statue's belt, so he worked from a *description* of the statue. Maybe the same description we read. You remember that, Records?"

Bob thought. "Well, it said the mask had yak horns, and the belt was hung with bells, rattles, grass, corn, roots—"

"Yes," Jupiter said. "Grass, roots, and corn! *Corn!*"

Mr. Chiang's eyes were wide. "Corn?"

"But," Mr. Clay said, "he put in the corn all right. I recall you said the ear of corn was still unmelted on the statue's belt, Jupiter."

"Yes, sir, and that was his mistake! I should have spotted it at once when we saw the statue in Jason Wilkes's house, but I missed it then. It wasn't until I saw that miniature ear of corn on the melted statue that I realized the truth."

Pete groaned. "What truth, First?"

"That the real Dancing Devil couldn't have had an ear of corn on its belt! The word *corn* is used in different parts of the world to mean different grains. To Europeans it means wheat. That art book we saw, fellows, was a British publication. When the author mentioned corn on the Devil's belt, he was actually referring to wheat! The corn we know is called maize by Europeans—because that's the American Indian word for it."

"Indians?" Mr. Clay said slowly.

"Yes, sir," Jupiter said. "What we call corn is native to America. Europeans and Mongols never saw an ear of corn until Columbus discovered America—*almost three hundred years after the Dancing Devil was made* in 1240 A.D.! The real Dancing Devil must have a sheaf of wheat on its belt, and the statue we saw destroyed was a fake!"

For a time there was only silence in the dim shack.

"But why?" Mr. Clay said at last. "Why make a replica? Who was wearing that Dancing Devil costume?"

Jupiter turned to look at Walter Quail.

"Mr. Quail?" he said. "You want to tell us?"

The thin assistant turned white. "I . . . I . . . No, I won't say—"

"A replica!" Chiang Pi-Peng said suddenly, his eyes blazing. "To fool me! To cheat my country! The fake was to be given to my country!"

"I think so," Jupiter agreed. "So that the real Dancing Devil would not have to be returned to China. Mr. Chiang is not an art expert, so the replica would have fooled him. But experts would see it in China. The replica had to be destroyed in front of witnesses so no one would know the real Dancing Devil still existed."

"Quail!" Mr. Clay thundered. "You'll pay for—"

"No, not Quail," Jupiter said, "although he has really known what was going on all along." The First Investigator turned sharply. "Hasn't he, Jim?"

"Me?" Jim Clay cried. "You're . . . You're crazy!"

Mr. Clay stared. "Jim? You mean my son is—?"

"Jim is the Dancing Devil, yes," Jupiter said grimly. "And Jim had the replica made. I should have guessed his involvement the moment we met Quail. Quail was genuinely surprised to find that the statue was gone—he'd probably seen it very recently. But when we came to the house, Jim had to hide it and say it was stolen, or we'd have known there were *two* statues!"

"You're wrong!" Jim Clay blustered. "I was locked in here!"

Jupiter shook his head. "When I went behind the shack, I found the loose boards you opened to get back inside after being the Dancing Devil. And I found this." He held out the belt of the Dancing Devil costume. There was a small pouch on it. He shook it, and a piece of chalk fell out!

"You finished leaving the trail of question marks while you were wearing the costume—and forgot to get rid of the chalk!"

Jim Clay looked at all of them. He turned to his father.

"I did it for you, Dad! So you could keep the Dancing Devil! So the Chinese wouldn't take it away from you!"

The youth slumped to the floor, as Mr. Clay shook his head unhappily.

21

Mr. Hitchcock Is Tempted

Several days later, The Three Investigators were in Alfred Hitchcock's studio office. The famous motion-picture director sat behind his massive desk, reading Bob's report on the boys' latest case. Finally he looked up with a frown.

"So Jason Wilkes had been bribed to help young Clay lead you on in his scheme to keep the statue?"

"Not at first, sir," Jupiter explained. "Jim's original plan was to give the replica to Mr. Chiang, steal it back, and have it smashed where Mr. Chiang would see it. But when we got involved, he decided to use us as the witnesses to the destruction of the statue."

"An unfortunate decision for him," the director observed with a twinkle in his eyes.

"Wasn't it!" answered Jupe with a chuckle. "Jim changed his mind about us several times, and finally made the wrong decision!"

"What do you mean?"

"Well, at the very beginning, when Jim was helping the little thief search for the lost replica on Pete's block, he tried to frighten us away. But since he couldn't find the statue himself, he had to let us lead him to it. Every time we seemed to be close, he tried to scare us off again so he could get to the statue first."

"He really thought he had it when the Chief said he'd sold the statue to Fritz Hummer," Pete put in.

"That's why we got locked in that cabin cruiser," added Bob.

"Oh?" said Mr. Hitchcock. "How did young Clay manage that?"

Jupe continued the story. "When he went to get his car outside the hobo camp, he called ahead to the thief and arranged for him to trap us in the boat—it was his father's yacht. But by the time Jim got to Hummer's shop, the thief had already discovered that the statue wasn't there any more. Jim had to let us out of the boat so we could help him trace it again. As soon as Hummer led us to Jason Wilkes, Jim was sure he'd reached the end of the search. That's when he decided to use us one last time—he didn't know his father and Mr. Chiang were on their way back to Rocky Beach that evening. He got rid of us for a while, bribed Wilkes to put on an act for us, and then cleverly led us on. He had Wilkes lock us up, called Quail in case we didn't get free ourselves, laid his trail, and prepared his Dancing Devil act in the canyon so we'd see the statue destroyed."

"It was melted in the sack already, of course," Bob said.

"He used a blow torch," Pete added.

"But once I realized it was a replica," Jupiter said, "I knew Jim had to be behind everything. He'd had time away from us to arrange for our capture in both the boat and Wilkes's house. He was separated from us, supposedly watching Hummer, when Pete saw the Devil at Wilkes's place. Our contact then was only through the walkie-talkies! And Jim was the one who insisted we all carry chalk."

"He also said he knew nothing of Oriental art, and yet he showed in Wilkes's house that he did," said Bob.

The famous director nodded. "A series of small errors you did well to analyze. But what of Walter Quail? He knew what was occurring, and yet did nothing to stop the young scalawag?"

"He couldn't, sir," Jupiter said. "You see, he was loyal to Mr. Clay, and didn't want Jim to get into trouble. He'd actually seen Jim with the little thief—that's why he was watching. He wanted to try to stop Jim, but he wanted to protect him, too. So he could say nothing to anyone. He could only try to stop Jim himself."

"So young Clay knew Quail would not inform the police or anyone, and took advantage of that," Mr. Hitchcock observed. "The young rascal!"

"Maybe just spoiled, sir," Bob said. "He knew that Mr. Clay hated to lose the Dancing Devil, and wanted to please him. He thought Mr. Clay would be glad. Maybe it's really all Mr. Clay's fault for not teaching Jim right."

"Perhaps," the great director said. "So, they were confounded by an ear of corn, eh? A knowledge of history can be important. Has that artist-thief been apprehended yet, by the way?"

"Yes, sir," Pete said. "He's admitted to making the replica."

"And what fate awaits all the scoundrels?"

"Well, Mr. Clay isn't going to press any charges," Bob said, "and he persuaded Mr. Chiang not to. But he's going to send Jim to work in one of his foreign oil fields—as an ordinary worker and on worker's pay!"

"To teach him that you have to earn your own way and work to get things," Jupiter explained.

"And Chief Reynolds is looking into other shady actions of the artist and Jason Wilkes," Bob said.

"Their future then, I expect, will not be bright," Mr. Hitchcock observed with satisfaction. "One point, my clever friends—I understand the use of chemicals to create the flame and smoke of the Dancing Devil's performance, but how did young Clay manage to fire that sack at such a distance?"

"He prepared the sack with a fuse and activated it by a radio signal," Jupiter said. "Jim was majoring in chemistry and electronics at college."

"Let us hope he will put his learning to better use in the future," the director commented. "And what of the real Dancing Devil? It was found safe and secure, and is now on its way back to China?"

"It was in Mr. Clay's cellar," Pete said, bending down and picking up a small black carrying case. "But we thought you might like to see it before Mr. Chiang takes it away."

He opened the case and set the barbaric little statue on Mr. Hitchcock's desk. It glistened green in the light, frozen forever in its wild dance.

"Magnificent," the famous director said in awe. "To think it was once held by the Khan of the Golden Horde! Take it! Go! Before I am tempted to try to keep it for myself!"

Grinning, the boys put the savage statue of the Mongol shaman back into its case and left the office.

Alone, Mr. Hitchcock began to smile. Even a Dancing Devil was no match for The Three Investigators. He wondered if his bright young friends would ever meet their match. Perhaps next time!

THE THREE INVESTIGATORS
MYSTERY SERIES

Calling all
MYSTERY FANS!

Keep your place with this Three Investigators bookmark! Just fold and tear on the perforated line.

Three Investigators
??? Mystery Quiz ???

If you can answer all three questions about The Three Investigators, you're an expert!

If you can't, you'll learn where to turn next for more excitement and suspense!

In which book did The Three Investigators . . .

1. meet a movie-star witch who casts deadly spells?

2. discover a fiendish gang of midget thieves?

3. see a creepy shadow that passes through walls?

(Answers on the back of this page)

The Three ??? Investigators Mysteries ???

THE
THREE INVESTIGATORS
MYSTERY SERIES
? ? ?

THE MYSTERY OF THE

Stuttering Parrot
Whispering Mummy
Green Ghost
Vanishing Treasure
Fiery Eye
Silver Spider
Screaming Clock
Moaning Cave
Talking Skull
Laughing Shadow
Coughing Dragon
Flaming Footprints
Nervous Lion
Singing Serpent
Shrinking House
Monster Mountain
Dead Man's Riddle
Invisible Dog
Death Trap Mine
Dancing Devil
Headless Horse
Magic Circle
Deadly Double
Sinister Scarecrow
Scar-Faced Beggar
Blazing Cliffs

THE SECRET OF

Terror Castle
Skeleton Island
Crooked Cat
Phantom Lake
Haunted Mirror
Shark Reef

**Random House Books
for Young Readers**

Answers to Mystery Quiz

1. The Mystery of the
   Magic Circle

2. The Mystery of the
   Vanishing Treasure

3. The Mystery of the
   Invisible Dog